Winter Sky

Winter Sky

Patricia Reilly Giff

A YEARLING BOOK

Text copyright © 2014 by Patricia Reilly Giff
Cover art copyright © 2014 by Shane Rebenschied/Shannon Associates

All rights reserved. Published in the United States by Yearling, an imprint of Random House Children's Books, a division of Random House LLC, a Penguin Random House Company, New York. Originally published in hardcover in the United States by Wendy Lamb Books, an imprint of Random House Children's Books, New York, in 2013.

Yearling and the jumping horse design are registered trademarks of Random House LLC.

Visit us on the Web! randomhouse.com/kids

Educators and librarians, for a variety of teaching tools, visit us at
RHTeachersLibrarians.com

The Library of Congress has cataloged the hardcover edition of this work as follows:
Giff, Patricia Reilly.
Winter sky / by Patricia Reilly Giff. — First edition.
pages cm
Summary: Almost twelve-year-old Siria, who chases firetrucks in the middle of the night to ensure her fire fighter dad's safety, learns about bravery one winter as she tries to mend a broken friendship.
ISBN 978-0-375-83892-7 (hardback) — ISBN 978-0-385-37192-6 (lib. bdg.) — ISBN 978-0-385-37193-3 (ebook) [1. Family life—Fiction. 2. Friendship—Fiction. 3. Courage—Fiction. 4. Fire fighters—Fiction.] I. Title.
PZ7.G3626Wi 2014
[Fic]—dc23
2013022399

ISBN 978-0-440-42179-5 (pbk.)

Printed in the United States of America
10 9 8 7 6 5 4 3 2 1
First Yearling Edition 2014

For Jillian Rose O'Meara,
my granddaughter,
with love

Once upon a time, before there was time, the night sky was dark. With no stars, there was nothing to see.

Coyote, that rascal, was bored. He was also clever. He went from burrow to nest, from the sands of the sea to the crests of the mountains. He gathered all the stars he could find in his backpack.

Not only was Coyote smart, he was a good friend. "Draw yourself in the sky with these stars," he told Big Dog.

Big Dog picked out a few; he trotted across the sky and drew his own picture: a star here, another one there.

Little Dog came next . . .

Then Orion.

Orion drew himself with a sword and a club.

Everyone had a turn.

Still stars were left in Coyote's backpack.

The pack was heavy, too heavy . . .

So Coyote reached up and threw the stars across the sky: red, yellow, and white, glowing blue.

He sat back on his haunches, satisfied. He'd rescued the night sky from the darkness.

CHAPTER 1

A blast of sound: the clang of sirens, the rumble of fire engines. Siria heard it clearly, even from their seventh-floor apartment.

She ran her fingers over Mom's star book, then tucked it under her pillow. Tonight was like the beginning of that coyote story: no moon, no stars, only flakes of snow rushing through the darkness.

She tiptoed across her room and opened the door an inch. Yes. Mimi, her sitter, was dozing on the pullout couch in the living room, her glasses still perched on her nose.

Siria grabbed her jacket off the desk chair and shrugged into it. She pushed up the window without a sound, bracing herself against the freezing air. The fire escape was slippery with ice. She imagined tumbling through the open stairs all the way down to the bottom floor. Dead as a doornail.

Toughen up, Siria.

She ducked outside and leaned over the edge. On the avenue below, a traffic light turned red, and a minivan screeched to a stop. The store windows were dim except for those at Trencher's Market, where red and green Christmas lights flashed on and off. Beyond the avenue, the sledding hills rose like pale pillows.

The sirens grew louder as the engines turned the corner onto the avenue. The minivan screeched again as it veered out of the way.

Siria slid down the icy steps, holding hard to the railing. Down one flight, her friend Laila's window, where she must be asleep by now. At the fifth floor, she stopped for a breath. Inside, Mr. and Mrs. Byars were watching the late-night news. A surprise. They were usually fighting.

On four, she angled around a pile of cracked flowerpots, then took a quick look into three, where Douglas lived. Douglas, with curly red hair he hated and kept hidden under a falling-apart baseball cap. Douglas, who loved working with his hands and said he'd build roads and houses one day. Douglas, her best friend since kindergarten.

She tapped on his dark window. "Hurry," she

whispered, and there he was, jacket on already, ratty blue baseball hat on backward.

He climbed out the window. "Yeow, freezing out here."

"Let's go," she said.

They raced down the last flights to the snowy sidewalk. That afternoon they'd jammed their bikes in behind the apartment-house fence, and now, in a moment, they wheeled them out and brushed off the snow.

They followed the fire truck, bent over the handlebars, splashing slush against the wheels. The truck turned and Siria pedaled faster, right behind Douglas, almost careening into Jason, the Trencher's Market delivery boy. He leaned against the store window with the teenage kid who followed him around like a shadow. Mike? Yes, that was his name. She could see the tattoo on the back of his neck, a dark *M* against his pale skin.

Siria's bike skidded, but she righted herself and called "Sorry" over her shoulder. They hadn't seen who she was. Lucky! If anyone knew what she was doing, she'd be in huge trouble.

Fire chasing!

Chasing Pop, a firefighter who rode high up on the ladder truck.

Following him to keep him safe. If only she could.

Look out for your pop, Siria. Had Mom said that long ago? Maybe it was a dream. She couldn't remember Mom, who had died when she was little. She had only the star book to remind her.

Pop was her whole family. She could picture him bending over his ship models, showing them to Douglas, who spent hours watching and sanding. Pop, who'd painted her room Easter-egg purple because it was her favorite color, and spattered gold on the ceiling for stars. Pop, who loved to laugh. He'd never been hurt at a fire, but still, Siria worried.

Ahead of them, the fire truck pulled to a stop. Wheels grazed the curb; lights flashed red against the snow.

Pop climbed down and rushed up the path of the old linen factory, Izzy right behind him. Danny and Willie, almost like twins in their turnout gear, began to work with the hose at the fire hydrant.

Siria leaned against a telephone pole, staying back with Douglas, hidden. She couldn't stop shivering. Snow had edged its way into the holes in last year's leopard boots, and wind blew her hair into her face. Next to her, Douglas waved his hands, trying to warm them. "No time to grab my gloves," he whispered.

She glanced around to see who else might be there: a few older people and four or five teenagers. One of them was Douglas's cousin, Kim, whose hoop earrings dangled almost to her shoulders.

Cool. Siria had earrings, too: tiny star studs that Pop had given her.

A stray dog stood on the corner. Siria had seen him around lately, sometimes even in her building's basement. He was fierce-looking, with matted hair, trailing a chain behind him.

Upstairs, a roaring sound! Windows shattered; sheets of glass flew out and smashed onto the street. One of the firemen ducked even though he wore his helmet and mask. Greasy black smoke poured from the openings, and orange-red flames shot out from the jagged glass. Siria clenched her fists deep in her pockets.

Piece of cake, Siria. Pop said that after every fire, hugging her to him, his eyes bloodshot from smoke and his dark hair smelling of it.

Pop, tall and rubber-band skinny, was a hero with two or three medals for bravery thrown in his dresser drawer. One was for rescuing a woman trapped in her car. The firefighters had used a set of instruments they called the Jaws of Life: cutters and spreaders had pried the doors apart and Pop had set the woman free. He never talked about the medals, though, except to say, "Rescue is the heart of firefighting."

He climbed the ladder now, while below, it took three others to hold the hose as water pumped through it, hitting the flames.

At last it was over. The fire sizzled and disappeared; smoke hung in ragged wisps. Siria could almost feel Pop's arms around her, his face filthy with soot.

Piece of cake.

He jumped back on the truck with the others, although she couldn't see Izzy, her favorite. The sirens were silent, but lights flashed as they pulled away.

People were leaving now, and Siria turned her bike to head for home with Douglas riding next to her, whistling, his red hair hidden under that backward cap.

She was glad she wasn't alone on the empty streets as they pedaled past houses and old factories, past the lots with rusted pipes and engines, past the old shed that tilted against the trees.

In a few hours Pop would be home, bringing warm cinnamon-raisin bagels from the all-night diner. His voice would fill the whole apartment. *Where's my girl?*

They'd sit at the table, sipping hot tea and buttering those crusty bagels. Pop would tell her about the fire while Siria leaned forward, listening, as if she didn't know about the red-hot flames, the smoke, and Pop on the ladder.

Now she looked toward their seven-story apartment house, its red bricks soft in the darkness, the bushes in front covered with snow. Home. Almost there.

It began to sleet; sharp bits of ice stung their faces.

She yelled to Douglas, "Thanks for coming with me."

"Love fires," he called back, grinning.

Siria couldn't wait to get home to snuggle under her quilt. Then she remembered that she'd left her window open. Her bedroom would be as cold as it was outside.

A coyote night.

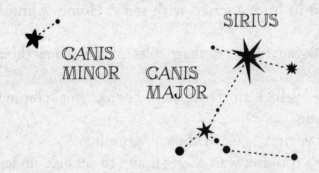

Head tilted, the mother stood on her balcony, watching the constellations.

The midnight blue above reminded her of her new daughter's eyes. And one star stood out among the rest; it glowed with white light, the brightest in the winter sky.

Men had been looking at that star for thousands of years. It gleamed as a perfect blue-white diamond in the collar of Canis Major, the Great Dog.

Its rising in Egypt marked the annual flooding of the Nile River.

Its appearance in the Greek sky announced the hot days of summer: the dog days.

Here, where the mother lived, only a glimpse of it could be caught in August. But in January it shone in the sky, huge and glowing, the month of her baby's birth.

The star was called Sirius.

"That's what we named our daughter," the mother said. "Siria, for the brightest star."

CHAPTER 2

It was late Friday afternoon, almost dark. Siria huddled on the fire escape with Laila from the sixth floor, her purple wool scarf pulled over her chin. They leaned against the brick wall, Laila's WIPE YOUR FEET mat pulled over their heads like a roof.

"What luck!" Laila said. "All this snow. No school until after the holidays."

Siria nodded. She didn't mind school the way Douglas did. He liked to be moving around, building things. And learning was hard for Laila in her special class down the hall. But during the holidays, Siria missed art and math, and her friends: Patti, who played the guitar, and Jilli, who drew wonderful pictures.

Too bad they all lived in different directions. Siria

wouldn't see them until after New Year's. Some-times they texted, but they usually forgot during the holidays.

Siria looked up at the gray sky now. "My twelfth birthday on New Year's Day!"

Laila nodded slowly. She took time to think about what people said; she took even longer to answer.

Siria grinned. Laila looked a little like an owl, with her glasses sliding down her nose and her mouth popped open to catch a snowflake.

"We'll see Canis Major, and Sirius, my star." Siria peered through the narrow spaces in the rusty fire escape. Blocks away were the white sledding hills and the creek that wound its way around them, a thin thread of water that had iced over.

Last summer, she and Douglas had spent days leaning against the picnic house, the creek in front of them with its overhanging branches. Tiny silver fish darted along the edge, and turtles the size of dinner plates sunned themselves on the rocks.

They'd built a sloppy wooden raft even though their feet touched the bottom. They'd stuck their heads in a pipe that hung out over the water, almost hidden in the long, reedy weeds. "Hello in there!" they'd called, their voices echoing back at them.

And they'd fished! Weeks of fishing, but there probably hadn't been anything big enough to catch since Pop was a boy.

Now, Jason, the delivery boy, and Mike, who followed him around, slid along on the frozen creek. They'd better hope the ice was solid.

"I know what you want for your birthday," Laila said. "A huge family, like Douglas's. That's what I want, too."

Siria nodded. Douglas, with his four brothers and a mom who made gallons of steaming cocoa on cold days for all the kids in the building.

"That family on TV," Laila added dreamily. "A mother, a father, a couple of kids, and even a horse."

And today was the beginning. A knife lay on the fire escape between them—not sharp, but it would have to do.

"Aunts. Uncles. Cousins," Laila said.

"You and I can join up to make a family," Siria said. "You have the mother, I have the father. We'll be the start of the kids. Douglas can be the brother. Too bad about the horse, though. It would never fit in the elevator."

Laila smiled. "I always wanted a horse."

Siria glanced up at the sky. "I've always wanted a dog. I'd carry her in my backpack. You'd never feel alone if you had a pet like that." She picked up the butter knife and slashed at her index finger. Not hard enough; no blood, not even a mark. She raised the knife again and plunged. . . .

Yeow.

She'd stabbed the edge of her boot. That didn't dent, either. "Wait." She pulled off her Christmas-tree pin. "We'll just use this."

"Right above my alley," Laila said.

"Up my alley," Siria said absently. They kept poking their thumbs but couldn't dredge up a bit of red. They stuck their hands together anyway. "Blood sisters," Siria said.

Just then, the noises began. They grinned at each other. The Byars in 5-D were fighting again. Plates would fly like Frisbees, glasses shattering.

It was as good as watching TV.

They raced down the fire escape, holding the ice-covered railing. Too bad Almo the super hadn't bothered with de-icer. How would Mrs. Gold, the old lady in 2-C, escape in an emergency?

Now came the tricky part.

On the fifth-floor landing, Siria slid onto the railing. With Laila holding her feet, she balanced herself on her stomach. It was very uncomfortable, but a prime way to watch Mr. and Mrs. Byars.

Mrs. Byars was gorgeous, with blond hair to her waist and bulging arm muscles; she was six feet tall, at least. And Siria wanted to be just like her.

Wait. She saw something interesting in 5-E next door. Siria wiggled out a little farther.

"Careful," Laila warned her.

Siria felt herself falling. "Help!" she yelled, and scrambled back.

A plate smashed, just missing the window and Mr. Byars. He ducked out of the way and peered outside. "It's those kids again!" he yelled to Mrs. Byars, forgetting she was trying to kill him.

Laila dragged Siria off the railing, and they raced back up to the sixth floor, sliding on the icy steps.

Siria sank down. "You will not believe what I just saw." She stopped for a breath. "The Wilsons must be moving out of Five-E. Most of the furniture is gone. But . . ."

She stopped, shook her head.

"That stray dog is in there, big as a wolf. He stared out the window at me, trying to scrabble outside. Whew. That would have been the end of me."

Laila poked at her glasses. "You're safe now. We just have to hope Mr. Byars doesn't tell our parents. My mother will have a heart attack if she knows I'm out here."

Siria pointed. "And your mother's coming up the avenue right now."

"See you." Laila ducked inside her window.

Siria made her way up one flight to her apartment. The day was really cold and getting windy.

She took a last look at the avenue. Far down, where the empty lots began, she could see the old shed Pop had helped build years ago. "This was a clubhouse when I was a teenager," he'd said, laughing. "We didn't know what we were doing. We all had splinters. The walls were crooked. I can't believe it's still standing."

Siria looked closer. Was it on fire?

Yes, maybe!

CHAPTER 3

Siria watched for a moment. Should she climb inside and call in the fire? Pop was in bed, off today, safe, but she wasn't sure it was a fire anyway. She saw smoke, but the shed was soaked with snow. How could it burn?

Besides, it was time for dinner. While Pop slept, Danny was cooking at the firehouse tonight.

She leaned against the railing. Even the smoke might be her imagination.

Still, Izzy's voice was in her head: *Small fires become big fires, become dangerous.*

Douglas was running up the avenue now. Was he staring back at the shed?

Siria cupped her hands around her mouth. "Hey . . ." She slid down the fire escape steps to meet him as he headed for his apartment on the third floor. "Did you see a fire?"

He shook his head. "All I saw was that decrepit Santa Claus in Trencher's Market." He pushed up the window, tossing the hat into his bedroom. One of his brothers, Ashton maybe, pulled him inside, laughing. "Some hat."

Siria climbed down the rest of the steps. She'd take a look at that shed. Danny wouldn't mind if she was late for dinner.

The sky was dark, with only a handful of stars, and once she passed the stores, the streets were dark, too. She ran, breathless when she reached the next corner.

She waded through the snow toward the shed. The bare branches of the trees around it were bent into weird shapes, charcoal gray against the sky.

The walls of the shed were rough pieces of wood with spaces in between; thin icicles hung from the low roof. She broke one off and sucked on it.

Footprints surrounded the shed, larger than hers, and wider. She followed them around the sides, kicking up soggy leaves and paper, black and sooty.

Soot! So there had been a fire.

She kept searching, picking up a scrap of thick green cloth. She turned it over. Wool from a jacket? Torn from a sleeve? She tucked it in her pocket, even though it was sopping wet.

She heard a rustle, a scraping against the wood, and froze. It came again, that whisper of sound. She peered between the boards. Someone was in there. A dark figure crouched on the floor.

Could he see her?

She turned, sliding, tripping over her boots, not caring about the noise she made. She had to get out of there. She scrambled through the snow until she reached the street. Safe.

Head down against the wind, she headed for the firehouse and dinner, talking herself out of being afraid. Imagination! *Probably no one in the shed. A fire from last summer, or the summer before.*

Besides, she was starving. The cafeteria lunch today, Meat Surprise, had tasted like leftover dog food. Only the cup of pale applesauce had been any good.

She'd thrown half of it away, while Mrs. W, the kitchen helper, scarfed down her third portion of the gray meat. "Delicious, Siria, right?"

"A surprise," she'd answered, not wanting to hurt her feelings.

Siria crossed the avenue now. The stray dog she'd seen in the empty apartment darted into the street against the traffic. Horns blared and a truck screeched, just missing him. Siria, hand to her mouth, watched as he reached the other side of the street, his chain dragging through a snowdrift.

It was only another block to the firehouse, which was squeezed between two high buildings, an apartment house and a dry-goods store that had closed years ago. The shiny red doors were high and wide for the trucks to move in and out.

Siria ran her fingers along the side of the ladder truck just inside, Pop's truck, Number Seventeen. It waited for him, ready to go, while he was home sleeping.

"Help, guys!" she said as she ripped open the Velcro ties on her jacket. "I need food!"

"Here she is!" Willie, Pop's best friend, called toward the kitchen in back.

By the time Siria had circled the other engines, Danny was pouring her a hot chocolate with foamy cream on top. A plate of hamburgers loaded with tomatoes and onions had already been set on the table for her.

"You have to keep up your strength, Siria," Danny said from the stove, raising his spatula. "And you're at the right place."

"True," Willie said. He loved to eat. He held a fat hamburger in one large hand and a cup of French fries in the other.

While she ate, Siria tried not to stare at the pencil marks that zigzagged up the back wall. They were bunched together, hardly getting higher.

Izzy measured her every September. "The wall is

crooked," she'd said last year, for comfort, when the line was only a tiny bit higher than the year before.

Siria knew she was a shrimp, the smallest kid in her class, and if you didn't count the four or five babies in her building, she was the shortest there, too, floors one to seven.

It was a miserable feeling, looking up at everyone, standing on tiptoe so no one would notice her height.

"Mom was a peanut, too," Pop had said once, his eyes soft. "But you should have seen her, Siria. Hands on her hips, not afraid to do what she had to do." He'd grinned. "And not afraid to tell everyone what she believed!"

Now Izzy squinted at her. "You're getting taller, Siria. I can see it with my own good eyes. Catching up to your pop!"

Izzy was the one who had given Siria the idea of hanging off the closet door every night. That was sort of what Izzy did: she used the firehouse as an exercise room, her wild dark hair swinging, arms reaching up, toes pointed down, face shiny with effort.

Izzy made everyone happy. On the opposite wall, she'd hung an old calendar that was torn off at July fourteenth. It had a picture of kids diving into a cool blue lake. "Isn't it fun to pretend it's summer all year long?" she'd said when she'd hung it up.

Now Danny reached over Izzy's shoulder and grabbed an oatmeal cookie. "With five kids at home," he said, "it's tough to get anything like this to eat."

He'd told Siria once, "You belong to the firehouse. We've known you since you were two months old, wailing louder than our sirens."

And Izzy had nodded. "She was a gorgeous baby, even with her mouth open like a canyon."

They thought they knew everything about her, but they didn't know about her fire chasing.

They sat at the table munching, everyone talking quietly because Jesse was dozing in the dormitory just beyond the kitchen, working his twenty-four hours on.

Danny and Izzy were talking about arson. Siria knew about arson: fires set deliberately, people hurt, firemen burned.

She leaned over her plate. The smoke at the shed—maybe that wasn't her imagination. Suppose . . .

Don't suppose, she told herself.

But what if someone had started that fire? It wasn't like the one they'd put out last night, caused by leaking chemicals.

But arson!

Don't let arson ever hurt Pop.

Or Izzy.

Or any of them.

CHAPTER 4

That night, Pop sat in the front room, gluing a tiny piece of canvas to his model ship's mast.

Siria leaned over him, resting her hands on his shoulders. "Great sail."

"I'm naming this one *My Star*."

"Ha. Not another *Siria*? We must have forty ships named *Siria*." She glanced at the shelves under the window. Yes, at least forty, lined up, crowded in, all beautiful.

Pop reached back to put his hand over hers. "You're my star."

"I know it." She kissed the top of his head and stopped in the living room for one of his huge books. The cover showed flames shooting up, spelling out the word *arson*. Her mouth went dry at the word.

She slid into bed and began to read. The first page

said that every fire had to be investigated. How had it started? She knew that from listening to Pop and Izzy.

Somewhere in the middle she read about kids and fires. A little kid who played with matches, not meaning to set a fire, wasn't an arsonist. It had to be deliberate: someone who really meant to do it. Sometimes arsonists even stayed to watch.

Siria couldn't stop thinking about the shed and who might have been inside. She shouldn't have left so quickly. One more moment and . . .

Go back. Go back now.

Too bad she was in her pajamas.

She looked over her shoulder. The light was out in the front room; Pop must be reading in bed.

Take care of Pop, Siria.

Mom would have done it.

Her jeans, her puffy jacket, and Mimi's knitted mittens and wool hat were all thrown on in a minute. She closed her bedroom door, then took baby steps through the living room.

Ten more tiptoed steps; then she opened the door an inch at a time, closed it silently behind her, and punched the elevator button for one.

Almo, the super, slept on the leather couch in the lobby that had worn itself into his shape. His shoes were off and his socks were full of holes. Mimi would say, "Not a very good image for the building."

Siria rushed past him, then rode her bike through the slush on the avenue. A dusty moon shone overhead, along with a sprinkling of stars. A food truck idled in front of Trencher's, and cars drove by, almost as if it were daytime.

Piece of cake.

She left her bike against a pole and clumped through the snow toward the shed, hardly breathing, putting each foot down as quietly as she could.

She reached the shed wall and felt the splintery wood against her fingertips. Inside, everything was still, but it was too dark to really see. She waited four minutes, maybe five. There was only one way to be sure. She had to open the door. She had to go inside.

Another minute.

She took a few steps around to the front. Listened. Ready to run, she put her hand on the door and pushed it open. She jumped back.

The moon lit the inside: an old quilt on the floor in the corner, food on a plate. In the center, a few pieces of half-burned wood and rolls of newspapers only half charred.

Someone had set a fire there.

Her heart began to pound. What had the book on arson said? Investigate. How had the fire started? She knew that now. Someone had started it with matches.

She looked at the empty lot, then closed the

door behind her. Straddling her bike, she headed for home, her mind whirling.

As she passed Trencher's, she saw a shadow in the doorway. She jumped, hands shaking, the handle-bars wobbling.

"Sorry," a voice called. "Didn't mean to scare you."

It was only Jason's friend, Mike. The one with the cool tattoo on the back of his neck.

Siria raised her hand to wave, then kept going. When she reached her building, she remembered the key to the outside door. It wasn't around her neck or in her pocket—it was dangling from the hook behind the kitchen door. She'd forgotten it again.

Almo was still asleep on the couch. It wasn't a good idea to wake him. He'd tell Pop she was wandering around at night, thrilled with his information.

She went around to the back, bypassing black plastic garbage bags with hats of snow, and leaned her bike against the fence. The basement door was always open, banging back and forth in the wind. Almo never closed it. What did he care about howling hurricanes, blizzards, or robbers on the loose?

She steeled herself to go down the ice-covered cement steps and sneak through the basement. Inside, it was almost completely dark. Kids with peashooters had used the lightbulbs for target practice again. Pieces of glass crunched under her feet.

Something went *bang* almost in front of her and her heart stopped for a second. Only the boiler in the electricity room!

She passed the laundry room. Half the washing machines didn't work, and the dryers didn't let off enough heat to melt an ice cream cone, so most people went across the street to Louie's Laundromat.

She remembered that huge dog who'd been in 5-E, the empty apartment. Sometimes he wandered in the open basement door. He might be hiding in the dark. "Gather your wits, Siria," she whispered; it was something Izzy said.

She tore through the basement toward the elevator and pressed the button, running in place in case the dog showed up and she had to race in the opposite direction and outside again.

And there he was! Eyes gleaming, his matted hair and thick tail brushing against the storage bins. But the elevator rumbled to a stop, and she was on her way before he moved. Upstairs, she grasped the apartment doorknob.

Don't be locked, please.

It turned and she tiptoed inside. The living room was dim, and the only sound was soft music coming from Pop's bedroom.

She couldn't wait to slide into her own bed and pull the quilt over her head.

But not yet.

She climbed up on the chair next to her closet door. *Raise those arms. Curl those fingers around the top of the door. Point those toes.*

Hang there.

Stretch!

It was painful, but she made herself stay pasted to the closet until she counted to one hundred ten, which was a nice round number and maybe would earn her a quarter inch.

She'd tried Pop's hand weights the other night but dropped them on her feet, causing angry purple marks across eight toes. Only the pinkies had escaped.

She finally slid under that warm quilt and tried not to think of the shed, and fire, and that huge dog with greasy fur and curved teeth.

She burrowed deeper into the quilt. If only she could tell Pop about the fire. But then he'd know she'd been outside at night, wandering around. How angry he'd be.

Think about the stars instead.

Think about the legends Mom collected.

Picture them.

She took a last look at her star book, then closed her eyes.

SIRIUS

CANIS
MAJOR

Singuuriq, an Inuit woman, lived in the cold Arctic north. Her little house rested beside a path that wandered from the earth to the moon.

She tried to do her work, but people passing by caused a draft that crept into the room, causing her seal-oil lamp to flicker and dance and the flame to turn bluish white.

The travelers were weary, thirsty. They needed to be rescued. She let them rest on the small bench outside her door. She held a cup of warm tea to their lips.

Singuuriq's seal-oil lamp still dances across the sky, twinkling, a diamond in Canis Major's collar. We call the diamond Sirius.

Today, astronomers say that stars don't twinkle. It's the earth's unstable atmosphere that makes it seem as if they do.

Singuuriq would shake her head at that.

CHAPTER 5

The next morning, Siria woke thinking of the little house resting between the earth and the sky.

She took a breath. A little house.

The shed!

She scrambled out of bed, threw on her clothes, and went to her bedroom window. She was going to watch the neighborhood, every minute, every second. If someone was setting fires, she'd find him. Or her.

Take care of Pop, Siria.

She went into the kitchen. Mimi was making granola with raisins, crunchy and sweet. She pattered around in homemade slippers and rollers in her hair, talking over her shoulder. "I heard about a constellation for you." She popped a raisin into her mouth.

Siria looked up from pouring juice.

"A unicorn with a crazy name." Mimi squinted up at the ceiling. "Monoceros."

Siria took a sip of pulpy orange juice, picturing a unicorn with a golden horn.

"He gallops between the Great Dog, Canis Major, and the Little Dog, Canis Minor."

"Ah, it's near Sirius, then."

Mimi smiled. "That's all I know. It can't be seen without a powerful telescope. But it's there."

That made Siria think about the shed again. Who had set the fire? And why? The answer was there somewhere.

Mimi cleared her throat. "So, Siria." She almost whispered, as if the room were filled with people. "Mr. Byars was in the elevator with me this morning."

Siria hoped her face looked innocent. She bit the insides of her cheeks.

"He said he'll call the cops if he catches you hanging out on the fire escape spying on them again."

Mimi's lined face was red. How worried she looked. Had Mr. Byars frightened her? He certainly frightened Siria.

Mimi went on. "He said you and Laila were leaning on your stomachs out over the street, trespassing, nearly killing yourselves."

Siria wanted to say "Mr. Byars doesn't own the

air outside his apartment," but Mimi was in a fragile state.

Fragile. She'd read that somewhere.

Mimi leaned forward and touched her ear. "Only one earring?"

Siria reached up. Oh no! She must have lost the other one. How could she have done that?

Someone banged on the apartment door. The noise was deafening. "That's Douglas," Siria said.

"Noise is that kid's trademark." Mimi tapped Siria's shoulder. "Promise me. No more hanging over railings."

"I guess."

Siria went into the living room and opened the door. "How about something to eat, Douglas?" Then her eyes widened. "What are you wearing?"

Douglas had shrugged into one of his older brother's jackets, probably Aydin's. It was much too big; the sleeves covered his hands. Gloves dangled over his fingertips.

"What took you so long?" He bounced on the balls of his feet. "Get your jacket. Get your gloves. I have to show you something."

"What about granola?"

"No time."

Siria called back to Mimi. "I'll eat later, thanks." And then to Douglas, "Why are you wearing that jacket?"

He shrugged. "Let's go."

She grabbed her jacket and wound a scarf around her neck. "I'll be back, Mimi." She followed him into the hall.

He kept going upstairs. "The roof."

"Why?"

"All you do is ask questions." He grinned at her and pulled open the heavy doors. They slid outside with a rush of frigid air.

"It's a birthday present for you." He waved his hands around until one of the gloves flew off.

She looked from one side to the other. Nothing was new on the roof except a pile of boards Almo had stacked against one wall.

"A present," she said a little uncertainly. She couldn't imagine what it was.

"You'll see."

She smiled at his freckled face, his dark eyes, the red hair escaping from his baseball cap. "You're such a good friend, Douglas. Thanks."

Siria glanced over the edge. The fire escape snaked down, glittering with ice and patches of snow. Across the avenue, the plastic Santa Claus in Trencher's window reached out to shoppers. Its costume wasn't red anymore; it was almost rusty brown. "No wonder," Pop had said once. "I remember that Santa when I was a kid."

Next door to Trencher's was Max's Art Supply

Store. Like Izzy, Max hated winter. In his window was a picture of a red sun coming up over a sandy beach.

"There's the dog again," Siria muttered. "Walking right past Trencher's."

"That one?" Douglas leaned next to her on the wall. "He'd take your leg right off."

"What does he eat? Who feeds him? Where does he belong?"

Douglas shook his head. "I don't think anyone takes care of him. Mr. Trencher might give him something, and maybe Jason. But pay attention. We have a lot to do."

She twirled around. "My present?"

Douglas's cheeks were red; his freckles stood out from the cold. He sank down on one of the boards. "It's freezing up here. We have to do something about that."

"Sure." She sank down next to him, head bent against the wind.

"We're going to build a star shelter." He blew misty breath out of his mouth. "For your birthday. Aren't we going to look for that constellation you like?"

"A star shelter! We'll see Canis Major, the Great Dog. And Sirius, the star in his collar. It's the brightest star in the winter sky. Oh, Douglas!"

He grinned. "You're always talking about it, so we'll sit up here in the dark turning into ice statues unless we build that shelter." He hesitated. "There's plenty of wood."

"But Almo . . ."

"Won't be up here until next May. He doesn't even clean the elevator."

Douglas was right. Siria smiled at him, then looked across the roof at the sledding hills blocks away and the frozen creek that ran along next to them.

Closer, she could see the shed, surrounded by those bare trees.

"Pay attention." Douglas wiped his face with his sleeve. "Where's Laila, anyway? She'd be pretty good at this."

"The dentist's."

He began to drag a board across the roof. "We'll pile them up on four sides and leave the top open. Nothing to it."

There was plenty to it. But why not?

"Aren't you worried about messing up Aydin's jacket?" She took one end of the board.

He rubbed a few splinters off the front. "He won't care."

"But where's yours?"

He waved his hand. "Who knows?"

They dragged another board across the roof.

"You're the best, Douglas," Siria said.

CHAPTER 6

It was late on Saturday afternoon. Siria was on her way to her teacher's house. Even though school had been let out early because of the snow, Siria wanted to wish Mrs. Hall a happy Christmas.

Mimi had helped Siria bake Christmas cookies that morning: tiny trees with green sprinkles, thumbprints with strawberry jam, and gingerbread men. They'd wrapped them on a plate with red cellophane and gold ribbon.

But Siria never got to Mrs. Hall's house.

At the far end of the avenue were boarded-up stores, with the old movie house looming high above them. Siria stopped to look at the window in front of the theater. A poster, faded and torn, showed an actress in an old-fashioned coat, her hair piled high on her head. She was probably a hundred years old by now.

Behind the poster, Siria could see inside: faded velvet chairs, maroon curtains, and . . .

Something was moving across the stage!

She leaned closer. That terrible dog—

How had he gotten in there?

He ran back and forth across the stage, almost as if he didn't know how to get down.

And then she saw the curl of smoke. One of the long curtains was on fire. She dropped the cookies and reached into her pocket for her cell phone. But it was on her dresser, forgotten at home.

The dog was barking now, howling.

She looked over her shoulder. No one in the street. People were far down, coming out of Trencher's, going into the dry cleaner's. Too far to hear her yell.

She yelled anyway.

The fire was stronger now. A second curtain had caught. Flames reached up.

A car came along the street. She waved. "Help, please! Call—"

The car slowed, then kept going.

The dog was trapped.

She tried to open the heavy front doors. Locked! The dog had jumped off the stage now; he was coming up the aisle toward her, but there was no way to help him.

A back door? There had to be. She ran to the corner and around to the alley. She heard her own hard breathing, felt her heart pound. The door! She rattled the knob, turned it, and it opened. A miracle.

Smoke rushed out at her and she bent her head. She couldn't go inside, she knew that much, but she called to the dog. "Come! This way!"

She took a step just inside the door, but it was hard to see. "*Get out,*" Pop would have said. "*Get out now!*"

The smoke swirled around her. Her throat was burning; she couldn't stop coughing. "Come!"

He raced along the aisle. She jumped away from him, but he paid no attention to her. He brushed past her, his eyes wild with terror, his mouth open, showing huge teeth. He ran down the avenue, waded through a drift of snow, and was gone.

And then someone's arms were around her waist, lifting her back and away from the smoky doorway.

"Breathe," he said.

She looked over her shoulder. It was Mike, the tattoo guy. "Thank you," she managed. At the same time, she heard the fire sirens.

"Engines coming," he said. "We can go now."

She was bent over, coughing. She wiped her face

with snow, then followed Mike down the street, and home, to drink water, lots of water.

And only then she remembered Mrs. Hall's cookies scattered in the snow. Ruined.

She wondered: Had the shed fire and the movie fire been set by the same person?

And did the scrap of green cloth in her pocket belong to him?

CHAPTER 7

She was dreaming about being guilty of something, she wasn't sure what, when something woke her the next morning.

It was just light. Snow was packed against the bottom of her bedroom window, and she crawled from under the quilt to look outside: cars drove along, Trencher's Santa Claus waved, and . . .

One of the fire trucks had stopped almost directly below. Lights flashed, but there were no sirens.

Pop was safe asleep in bed, but what about Izzy? Izzy, with her wild hair and great smile, her hugs that were so tight it was hard to breathe. What about Willie, who made the best dinners, and Danny, who had five kids? What about everyone at the firehouse?

She had to make sure they were safe.

She searched for her leopard boots. What a waste of time! Her room was a total mess, with papers and pajamas and Tootsie Roll wrappers and mittens that didn't match scattered all over. Someday soon she'd clean the whole thing up. She'd be as neat as they were at the firehouse. Their pants were rolled down over their boots so they could just step into them, ready to climb on the truck in seconds. She had to remember that for her own fire chasing.

One boot was under her bed, the other halfway out of the closet. She pulled them on and tiptoed down the hall, listening to Pop's heavy breathing.

She slipped out the apartment door and into the hall, then punched the elevator button, but someone had jammed it up again.

She took the stairs, the lights dim over her head. Was she the only one awake in the whole building?

Outside, the fire truck had stopped in front of Trencher's Market. A ladder leaned against an ancient tree. A few crumpled brown leaves still clung to the branches that stretched over the cracked sidewalk.

Izzy was perched on top of the ladder, but there wasn't any fire, or even smoke.

Danny and Willie were looking up, hands on their hips. "Go, Iz!" Willie called.

Siria zigzagged closer to them, looking up, too.

"Up early," Danny said.

She nodded. It was great to fire chase in the daytime—no hiding. But there wasn't really a fire. Up high, on the tip of a branch, was a little black cat. She arched her back like a leftover pinup from Halloween. One paw was extended, ready to scratch.

As Izzy reached out to grab her, she moved to the next branch. But Izzy was faster, and then the cat was in her arms, climbing up on her shoulder.

Danny grinned. "What a rescue!"

"Sharp claws," Izzy called on her way down.

Siria waved, then went back upstairs. Pop was awake, sitting at the kitchen table, turning the pages of his newspaper. "I thought you were asleep." He patted the chair next to him.

"Izzy just saved a kitten from that half-dead tree outside."

"That's the best part of firefighting. The rescue."

She slid into the chair and reached for a bagel. "Even a kitten?"

"Anything that's alive. To do something for someone who needs help. It's a great feeling." He gave her shoulder a gentle squeeze and went back to his newspaper.

What about that poor dog, wandering around with no one to feed him? How thin he was. Even with that matted hair.

The dog was starving.

She took time buttering the bagel. Suddenly she wasn't hungry. She took a couple of bites, then went into the bedroom to reach under her pillow.

She pulled out the small book with the soft green cover where Mom had written down some of the old legends, and stories she'd imagined herself, about the constellations.

Once, Pop had said, "Mom and I would sit out on the balcony, holding hands, looking up at the winter sky, even when it was freezing."

Siria searched for one of the stories, one she could hardly remember. She stopped to read about the Milky Way with its millions of stars splashed across the dark. On another page, Mom had written about huge planets turning and tilting, and bursts of fire as stars streaked through the sky.

But that wasn't what Siria was looking for. It was something near the beginning of the book.

Mom was telling her exactly what to do, no matter how impossible it seemed.

And hadn't Pop told her that rescue was everything?

She had to do it. She had to save that fearful dog.

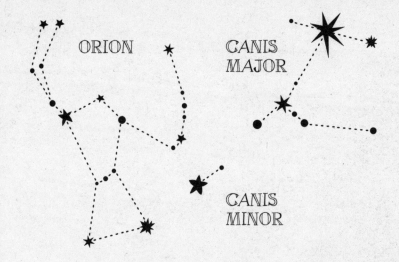

ORION   CANIS MAJOR

CANIS MINOR

Orion was a mighty hunter, but a scorpion scuttled into the folds of his cloak and stung him! The poison went through the hunter's body, paralyzing . . .

Killing.

How sad it was for Diana, goddess of the hunt, to see Orion there, all the fight gone out of him. She had to help him!

She carried him up high into the sky, among the stars.

His sword hangs from the three bright stars on his belt. His club is raised in one hand, and the pelt of a great lion he killed dangles from another.

With him are his two companions: a great dog with a gem star called Sirius in his collar, and a smaller playful dog. They travel around the sky together.

CHAPTER 8

It was one thing to grab a small cat with sharp little claws, but another to rescue a massive dog that looked like a wolf.

Siria shivered. Maybe Laila would help. Or Douglas.

But right now, she and Laila were on their way to the firehouse to see the cat. They rushed into the elevator, stepping over someone's stale doughnut. The walls were one big mess of graffiti. "Very colorful." Laila twirled around to admire all of it.

Someone had written *Mery Christmas*. "The graffiti artist didn't know how to spell." Siria rubbed at the red and green paint, probably stolen from Max's Art Supply Store.

Outside, they waved to the dry cleaner guy, then

passed Mr. Trencher outside his store. "I'm breathing in the cold air," he called. "I smell snow on the way."

"Me too!" Siria yelled back.

She and Laila swung hands as they crossed the avenue and passed the school. Presidents' heads, molded in cement, poked out of the walls near the roof.

Siria almost felt sorry for George Washington— the top of his head had turned into a pigeon's nest, and a mess of white bird gloop made one shoulder a couple of inches higher than the other.

Past the school, she could see the shed roof. If only she could talk to Pop. But it would be the end of her fire chasing. She'd be up all night, sitting at the window worrying about him.

No, she had to work on this herself.

"What's the matter?" Laila asked.

Siria shook her head. She reached into her pocket and pulled out the scrap of green cloth. "I found this."

Laila ran her hands over it. "From someone's jacket?" She shook her head. "I've seen it before. I almost know . . ."

But they were at the firehouse now, reading the sign on the door: CAT FOUND in Izzy's bold printing. DESPERATE FOR A HOME.

Jesse poured hot apple cider while the cat, tail

held high, jumped up into the open door of the rescue engine. She padded around the jacks and air guns that could slice through metal until she found an empty spot and folded herself into a ball.

"Want a kitten?" Jesse asked from the stove.

"I'm allergic," Laila said. "To cats. To dogs. Sorry."

Siria looked down at the carrot cupcake Jesse had put in front of her. Laila allergic! She couldn't help with the dog even if she wanted to.

Izzy swooped down to sit at the table. She poured her own cider and leaned back. "I never had a cat." She ran her hands through her long thick hair. "Just for now, until someone gives her a home, I'm calling her Smoky."

It would be great to have a cat, but Siria knew Pop would never say yes to a real pet. "The most I could deal with," he'd said once, "are hermit crabs and a couple of guppies."

How could you count them as pets? They just hung around in aquariums, not paying attention to anyone outside their world. How could you hug a hermit crab?

Siria looked around the table at the firefighters. What would they think if they knew about the shed fire? And that whoever started that fire might have started the movie fire, too? How would they feel about Siria's not telling?

On her way out, Siria reached into the front seat

of the rescue truck to touch the sleeping cat, its face hidden in its thick tail. Siria looked back at Izzy. "That was a great rescue."

"My specialty." Izzy winked.

By the time Siria and Laila reached their building, a stinging snow had begun, almost sleet, pattering over the streets and sidewalks. Laila shuffled her feet in the snow. "I've just decided. I'm going to ask for a couple of fish in a tank. Not as good as a horse, but they'll be happy when I feed them."

"They will," Siria said.

"I'm going to ask for a trip to the Rocky Mountains, too." Laila grinned. "I'll get a trip to my aunt's house in Delaware instead. Almost as good."

Inside, Siria left Laila on the sixth floor and went up to her own kitchen. Pop was napping because he'd be working later tonight, and she opened the cabinets quietly, trying not to wake him.

She stared at the shelves. She'd never had a dog. What did dogs eat, anyway? Probably not red beets, or baked beans, original or home-style. And certainly not a jar of applesauce or peaches.

The dog would probably eat anything, but it wasn't fair to give him something that might make him sick. Siria leaned her head against the cabinet. If only she hadn't read Mom's story about Orion.

She reached into the grocery-money cup and scooped out a bunch of change. She'd buy something suitable for a ravenous dog. On a bitter snowy day like this, he might be in the basement. She put a can opener in her pocket and went outside.

A moving truck was parked at the front door, and two guys were lugging a couch outside. Their hair was covered with snow, and so was the couch. It was probably from apartment 5-E.

Inside Trencher's, Christmas music blared: *"Walking in a winter wonderland . . ."*

Jason leaned against the counter, talking to Mike with the tattoo. They stopped to wave at Siria. She wanted to thank Mike for helping her at the movie the other day, but he shook his head. Maybe he was embarrassed in front of Jason, so she just smiled.

In the pet aisle, Siria found a pyramid of dog food cans: beef, lamb, chicken, and vegetables. "Dogs eat beef like crazy," Mike said, behind her now. "They love it."

"All right." She took a couple of cans and some cardboard bowls.

She plunked down the money and trudged around the apartment house, mounds of snow covering the path. Someone had strewn bread crusts around, probably Mrs. Gold, and sparrows swooped down, starving.

Siria went in through the open basement door. A woman was singing in the laundry room, her voice low and sweet. Mrs. Byars? *"Sleigh bells ring. Are you listening?"*

"I'm listening," Siria whispered. Not alone after all.

She edged her way down the aisle between the metal storage bins, then opened a can of beef. "Here, dog." She didn't hear him. Was he there? Maybe he could smell its horrible meaty smell. Yuck!

She took a few steps away from the laundry room and the woman singing. She could run back if she had to, but as long as the woman kept singing, she was safe.

She saw him! At the end of the bins, the dog stared at her. Fur wet and matted down, he was panting, teeth gleaming.

Siria moved back against the wall. He was almost as big as she was. She dumped the beef into one of the cardboard bowls, hands shaking, and pushed it away from her on the floor.

He strained to get to the food, his claws scrabbling against the cement. He was panting harder, desperately. Why couldn't he reach it?

Even in the dim basement light, Siria could see how hungry he must be. Ah, the end of the chain around his neck was caught between the wall and the end bin. He was trapped there.

How to help without getting too close?

Siria pushed the food toward him with one foot.

He began to eat as she darted forward, yanking out the chain.

"You're free."

He stopped eating and looked up.

Only a faint hum came from the electricity room; the woman had stopped singing. Maybe she was gone. Siria took a breath, her heart in her throat. She rushed toward the elevator, tripping over an empty box, and pressed the button.

The elevator was right there. She slid in and leaned her forehead against the *Mery Christmas* graffiti to catch her breath.

The elevator stopped on the first floor. "What's the matter with you?" a voice said.

Douglas stepped in, carrying a shopping bag.

It was too much to tell him everything. "I just . . . Let's get out of here."

He punched the button for three, and she saw his hands: raw, red, and thumbs blistered. "Douglas! What happened . . . ?"

For a moment he didn't answer. Then he grinned. "I was moving the boards. Without help."

"I'm sorry. Really . . ."

He waved one chapped hand. "Don't worry."

She pictured the dog that needed to be fed.

Desperate.

She had a lot to worry about.

CHAPTER 9

Wind swept across the fire escape outside the kitchen windows and rattled the panes.

"It's cozy in here, though." Mimi slid a warm platter of curly pasta twists onto the table, and then hot rolls and butter. She raised one shoulder. "But I don't know about the dessert. A chocolate ice cream sundae? On a night like this?"

"Love it," Siria said.

"Now, Christmas," Mimi said. "I wish I knew what to knit for your father. Socks? A quick scarf, maybe?"

Siria bent her head, hiding a smile. Pop had dozens of Mimi's socks in his drawer, and four or five scarves hanging from hooks in his closet. "He'll be happy with anything."

"Slippers for Izzy," Mimi said. "I know that."

Izzy was always part of their Christmas. She'd take Siria shopping on her next day off and help trim their tree.

Mimi waved Siria away when it was time for dishes. Siria blew her a kiss. "You're the best," she called as she went into her bedroom.

The wind blew against her window, moving the curtains. It was bitterly cold out, a night to read her mother's star book under her quilt. The sky was dark, with only a pale moon over the sledding hills, and the creek was a strange color. It didn't glimmer with that blue-white ice as it had before dinner.

It was red.

How could that be?

Siria pulled the quilt around her, opened the window, and stuck out her head.

It was hard to see with the wind in her face. She pushed her hair out of her eyes.

It was a reflection. Glowing. Shimmering against the frozen creek. She could see it clearly now, marked by two willows that leaned out over the water.

She pulled her head inside, shivering, and closed the window. She sank down on the floor, trying to think. What did it mean?

A fire, close to the creek. But what was there to burn? Only the small room that sheltered the picnic tables in the winter. And the snow there was so deep.

She swallowed. Mimi would be busy in the kitchen for another ten minutes; then she'd sit in the living room, feet up, knitting, her needles clicking. There was no way to get past her.

It would have to be the fire escape, covered with snow, slippery. . . .

And what about that wind? There was no help for it. She tugged on an extra set of jeans, two sweaters, and her leopard boots, which lay under her bed.

"I'm going to shower, Mimi." She crossed her fingers and went into the bathroom to turn on the water just a bit. Then she climbed out her window, sliding along as quickly as she could, holding the icy railing.

She tried to duck as she reached the sixth-floor landing. Laila would only slow her down. But there she was, doing ballet steps near the window. She stopped on one foot when she saw Siria. "Wait for me." She looked back over her shoulder, then grabbed her jacket off the chair. "It's freezing out. Where are we going?" she asked, her head out the window.

"The creek," Siria said a little reluctantly.

"Ice-skating? I have to get my skates."

Siria shook her head. "No skates. Just hurry."

They stopped at Douglas's floor. Ashton and Aydin were wrestling on the rug. "Hey," Siria yelled in.

"He's not here." They rolled away, pounding each other.

"If I had a brother," Laila called, "I'd know where he was."

They circled the last landings and jumped to the ground. It was a long walk; snow crunched under their boots and coated their shoulders. No engine lights flashed in the distance; no sirens wailed. No one else had called in the fire.

Laila stopped. "Why are we rushing down to the creek if we're not skating?"

"No time." Siria took her arm. "Just wait till we get there."

At last they reached the creek and stood on the rocks at the edge. "Poor fish under all that ice. They can't even see the sky." Laila's teeth chattered. "What are we doing here, anyway?"

Siria brushed snow off her face with her glove. She leaned forward. "Someone is setting fires."

"Here?" Laila's eyes widened behind her glasses. "Call your father!"

If only she could. But she'd have to tell him about going out at night. What would he say? What would he think? "Let him know I'm wandering around? I can't do that."

"You could call the fire department without giving your name," Laila said slowly. "No one would have to know it was you."

Siria tapped the cell phone in her pocket. "What about caller ID? They'd know. Everyone knows me." She shrugged, feeling a little sick over it.

Laila tilted her head. "Maybe I could call."

"Don't do that. Let's wait and see."

Laila nodded. "But let's get out of here."

"In a minute. We're okay, really." She wondered if that was true. She walked around the willows, their thin limbs swaying. What could have caused that reflection?

In front of the picnic house, she found a plank of wood like the ones Almo had dragged up to the roof, but this one was charred.

"You're right," Laila said. "There was a fire."

Siria pulled off her gloves and reached out. It was hot, still smoldering.

Someone had wedged paper bags underneath, although most of the paper was gone now.

"Who . . ." Laila stood behind her, touching her shoulder.

Siria glanced around. There was only the sound of the wind, the cracking of ice, and branches rustling. The creek was half hidden by rocks. Anyone could be hiding, watching them. They'd never hear him. He could come right up to them and . . .

Laila pulled her sleeve. "Let's go back. Please."

Still, Siria looked down at the board. Why would anyone set a fire here?

"Siria?"

"I'm coming."

They turned and went back to the apartment. Siria looked over her shoulder once or twice. But singing came from the church on the avenue, the choir practicing "Silent Night." Not like tonight, with the whoosh of the wind and car horns blaring.

The traffic light changed; Jason and Mike crossed from the other side of the street. Mike wasn't wearing a hat. In this weather! But then she saw that cool tattoo on the back of his neck. Of course, he was showing it off. The dog, looking meaner and scruffier than ever, followed, a half block away.

"Siria," Laila said slowly, "I think I know who set that fire."

CHAPTER 10

"That green cloth you found? It belongs to Douglas," Laila said. "It's part of his jacket."

Laila was right. "Even so, you can't believe . . ."

"Good people can do bad things," Laila said slowly.

"Not Douglas."

"He loves fires. Remember the time he set one in his bathtub? And another, down in the lots . . ."

Siria put her hand up. Shook her head. "That was a long time ago. We were in first grade."

"You know it," Laila said. "Remember?"

"Don't."

The wind was strong, and they were silent as they climbed the fire escape.

Laila let herself in her window. "I'm sorry, Siria," she whispered. "Really sorry."

Siria didn't answer. She turned and went back down the fire escape, feeling the terrible wind and cold through her jacket. She'd talk to Douglas, ask him. He'd tell her . . .

Never mind what he'd say. It wouldn't be about setting fires.

She stopped at his window. She could see Douglas standing in the living room, wearing his brother's jacket, his hat wet from snow. He'd been outside, then. At the creek?

His brothers must be fighting. Yelling again. Kevin, loudest of all. "Are you trying to kill us, Douglas?"

She leaned against the wall.

"What's Mom going to say when she sees that stove?" one of the brothers shouted. "Soot all over the place. If we weren't here, the whole kitchen might have gone up in flames."

She didn't wait to hear the rest. She scrambled upstairs. *Just a coincidence*, she told herself over and over. But still she was crying.

She didn't bother hanging from the closet. What was the use? She hadn't grown a speck in months. She huddled under the quilt, but she couldn't get warm; her hands and feet were numb.

She closed her eyes, but it took forever to fall asleep.

✦

In the morning, she stood at her bedroom window, looking at the sledding hills and the creek, white with drifts of snow. She pictured Laila's earnest face, her glasses sliding. Laila, who never lied, who always tried to think things out.

And Douglas's hands . . .

Blistered.

Red.

Burned?

Hadn't he thought about small fires growing larger?

Growing dangerous?

Hadn't he remembered helping Pop with the model ships? And what about Izzy, or Danny and his children? Hadn't Douglas thought about Willie and Jesse playing ball with him all last summer?

She threw on her clothes and went into the kitchen.

Mimi was scrambling eggs with bits of tomato and bacon tossed in the pan. But Siria could manage only a few bites.

"Are you all right alone for a while?" Mimi asked.

"Sure."

"I want to go across to Trencher's. He was supposed to have the groceries delivered, but that boy is never around when you need him."

Siria kept nodding. She had to make herself

go down to the basement and feed the dog. And then . . .

She'd go up to the roof to see Douglas.

A word was in her head. A bitter word.

Arson.

Siria bent over to look at the cans of dog food under her bed. Chicken and rice. Beef. She took them both.

As the elevator passed the third floor, she caught a glimpse of Douglas in the hallway, bouncing his ball against the wall.

He didn't look like an arsonist. He looked more like the brother she wanted. She brushed at her cheeks angrily and stepped out when the elevator reached the basement.

The dog wasn't there—not in the laundry room, not in the storage bin aisle. She even tiptoed to the electricity room, where machinery hummed. The back door was open, so maybe he'd wander in later.

She dumped the chicken onto the paper bowl and left the other can on top of one of the storage bins. Lucky. She hadn't had to go near him.

She walked all the way up to the roof. What would she say to Douglas? She didn't open the heavy door but stood beside it, head against the wall. *Stop crying.*

Crying? Over a fire starter?

She tore open the door.

Douglas was bent over the beginnings of the star shelter. Boards were piled on one side, high enough to sit against. He'd just started the second side with two boards laid end to end.

Siria could hardly breathe. She ran toward the star shelter and kicked the finished side. She pushed the top board off, and the next.

Douglas spun around. "What are you doing?"

She kept kicking at the boards. She was crying so hard, she could hardly talk. "You. Setting fires," she managed.

"Stop!" he yelled.

"Your jacket. I know."

He shook his head.

"Your hands."

He put them behind his back.

"You were almost my brother." She put her thumb to her mouth and felt blood from a splinter. "I'll never talk to you again."

He stepped back. "What are you talking about?" His face was blotched, and she saw that he wasn't really looking at her.

"I'm going to watch you," she said. "Every second. One more time and I'm going to tell."

She stopped for a breath. "I'll tell Pop and Izzy. I'll go to the station house and tell the police."

"You've lost it." Now he kicked at the shelter. He was stronger than she was. The boards fell apart, and in moments, all of it was destroyed.

She went back toward the roof door, but it was locked. Over her shoulder, she saw Douglas climbing down the fire escape.

She waited until he was gone, her hands tucked in her jacket.

She tried to lift one of the boards, to begin the shelter all over again. It wouldn't work. Even with Laila's help, it would be too hard.

If only she were taller. Stronger.

She looked over the edge of the building. Douglas was gone. Down on the avenue, Jason straddled his bike, packages in his basket. It was a busy morning, with cars bumper to bumper and people wandering on the street.

No dog down there.

Had Douglas paid attention to her? Would he stop? No more fires?

She'd have to stay up all night to be sure.

Maybe she'd hide somewhere on the avenue. If Douglas came out of the building, she'd see him and follow.

She went down the snowy fire escape slowly,

Douglas's footprints ahead of hers. She let herself into the apartment. Without taking off her jacket, she reached for Mom's book, ran her fingers over the soft leather cover, and opened it. She remembered the story of best friends.

What would Mom say to all this?

GEMINI

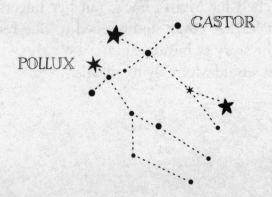

CASTOR

POLLUX

Castor and Pollux grew up together. Some say they were twins, others that they were half brothers. They were the best of friends.

Sometimes they fought, jumping to conclusions, and one would blame the other. The arguments didn't last long, though, and they had many adventures together.

One day, when freeing a herd of cattle, Castor was killed. Pollux was heartbroken.

But Zeus rescued them. He sent them high into the sky, where they can be seen during the winter months. They stand with their feet in the Milky Way, always together.

CHAPTER 11

If only she and Douglas could be friends again. If only he hadn't set those fires.

She spent the rest of the afternoon in the kitchen with Mimi. The apartment smelled of cinnamon-and-sugar cookies baking in the oven. Trays of gingerbread men and buttery Santa Clauses filled every countertop. Siria and Pop would bring them to the firehouse tomorrow. She filled another plate for her teacher, too.

After dinner, she went down to the basement. The food was still there, a sticky mess. The dog hadn't come back, then. Suppose he was caught somewhere with that chain he dragged behind him?

In bed later, she wondered: Was he trapped out in the cold and the snow? Hungry, with no way to get food? Such an ugly, unfriendly dog. Would anyone ever stop to help him?

Don't think about it.

She must have dropped off to sleep, but then she heard the sirens.

A dream?

She sat up to listen to the wail as they came closer. The sound was real, and Pop was on duty.

Siria rolled out of bed and crouched at the window, the pane cold against her forehead. She caught a glimpse of the engine, huge and misty red against the sky as it turned the corner.

The sirens cut off; the fire had to be nearby.

Siria stood up and opened the window. The smell of greasy smoke drifted up from the street, where two or three people were running by.

She glanced at the little clock on her dresser; it flashed twelve. Midnight. She threw her jeans and jacket on over her pajamas and toed into her boots.

In the living room, Mimi was sound asleep on the pullout couch, breathing softly, her head resting on her shoulder. A ball of gold wool had let loose, cascading across the floor.

Was that going to be a Christmas present for her? Siria closed her bedroom door. No time to wait for the elevator.

She flew down the fire escape, passing Laila's darkened window, hesitating at the third floor. Douglas's floor.

Was he there, or somewhere outside? Would he have dared start tonight's fire? She peered in. Dark. Too bad they wouldn't go after the trucks again.

She didn't bother with her bike. More people were running now; doors were opening; someone was yelling. She turned the corner to see another factory on fire, its painted walls stained black. Ashes drifted through the air like gray snowflakes.

Someone said, "Old wires. I always knew it would happen."

Siria took a breath. Maybe it wasn't arson this time.

Engines lined up along the curb, red lights pulsing onto the snow. Firefighters moved around the trucks, calling to each other as Willie and Izzy unwound the hose.

More trucks pulled up; the dispatcher had called in a second house for help. That meant a three-alarm fire: hot and dangerous.

One of the firefighters was up on the roof with an axe, breaking the tiles, trying to make an opening for the smoke and fire to escape. Close to the building, the ladder went up and up, then stopped at the top floor, bumping gently against the wall just below one of the windows.

Siria looked for Pop's lucky number, seventeen, on the side of the truck, but even though she couldn't see it, she knew it had to be his.

A pair of ambulances drove up, sirens screaming. People moved away to give them room. Through the smoke, Siria saw Mrs. Byars from the fifth floor, her hand to her mouth. And Patti from school, huddled next to her mom.

Was Douglas somewhere watching?

Siria turned, staring into faces, standing on tiptoe to see past the knots of people. Douglas wasn't there, but she saw his brother Kevin.

Pop's voice was in her head as he grasped the bottom of the ladder: *Nothing to worry about, Siria. Climbing is a piece of cake.*

And he was always right.

Always.

If only Pop were a teacher, or had an art store like Max's. Anything but a fireman. He'd be home at night, and they'd watch TV while he worked on his ship models or filled in the newspaper crossword puzzles with a sharp pencil.

The ambulance sirens cut off, but the turret lights kept turning slowly as the drivers pulled in closer, waiting.

Pop began to climb.

"It must be at least eight stories," someone whispered, and Siria counted the line of windows. Yes, eight.

Pop stopped halfway. Catching his breath? He began to climb again.

A man reached out of the highest window, the fire behind him like a torn orange curtain. He must have been terrified of the terrible heat, throat dry, eyes burning from smoke.

Pop's eyes were so often bloodshot from smoke. He'd rub them, tilt his head back, using eyedrops from the medicine cabinet.

Now he stood at the top of the ladder, right under the window, reaching for the outstretched arms, moving in closer, grabbing for him.

And then the man was on the ladder with him!

"One of the security guards," Mrs. Byars said behind Siria.

So much noise! The steady rumble of the engines, the fire crackling as a board broke loose and slammed onto the cement. Still, she heard a soft sound from the people around her beginning to breathe again.

Pop and the man were coming down.

Pop was safe.

Piece of cake, Siria.

But Pop wasn't finished. As soon as he and the guard reached the bottom, he turned and started up again, three firemen holding the heavy hose as it sprayed water high across the building.

Siria sank on the ground, the wet snow under her, hands to her mouth. Why was Pop going up again? No one was at the window; the flames weren't as strong. Water from the hose streamed into broken windows.

Another firefighter went up behind him, fast. Even in all that gear, Siria was sure it was Izzy, quick and light. Pop climbed inside the window, Izzy right behind him.

How long were they in there?

She must have said it aloud; someone beside her whispered, "It's only been a minute or two."

She remembered the summer night when Douglas had dared her to go with him on the huge roller coaster at the carnival.

They'd sat in front, where they could see the tracks, and she'd been terrified at the dizzying height.

It took forever for the car to lumber to the top; then they were stuck there endlessly until their car plunged almost straight down, Siria's heart with it.

The ride went on and on, Siria's hands gripping the rail.

When at last the ride was over, a girl said, "Only a minute and a half. What a gyp!"

How strange that time could expand or contract like that.

Pop and Izzy were still in there—it was forever. Siria comforted herself. They carried personal alert systems. If one of them stopped moving, the alarm would go off, and other firefighters would rush to find them. Their turnout gear was fireproof, and their air tanks had almost a half hour of oxygen.

None of that helped. She wanted Pop and Izzy out of there.

But at last, Izzy was at the smoky window, Pop behind her. They were slow coming out; Pop was helping someone. . . .

"Ah," Mrs. Byars said. "The other guard."

One of Pop's hands held on to the ladder, his other arm around the man he held. One foot reached for a step, then the other.

Halfway now, Izzy right behind him.

Go home. Before Pop sees you here.

What if he found out about the fire chasing? How could she tell him she needed to be there, to be his luck?

Could she say she was afraid to lose him, that she was afraid to be alone? No matter what she said, it would be the end of her going out at night.

They were almost at the bottom, and the guard jumped off the ladder. Another board from the roof teetered high over Pop's head.

Everyone below gasped.

The board was falling, and Pop was underneath.

CHAPTER 12

One ambulance pulled away with the security guard, but Pop lay on the ground, surrounded by the other firefighters.

The engine lights kept flashing; the radio crackled. Danny, Jesse, and Izzy bent over Pop. Izzy's helmet and mask were off. Her face was filthy.

Siria pushed her way over, bumping into people, whispering "Sorry." Jesse tugged at her shoulder. "Siria! Just stay back. Wait."

She scrambled away from him, darting around everyone until she was squeezed in as close as she could get.

Helmet off now. Blue eyes. Streaked face.

He was alive!

Her heart began to beat again.

He saw her, too. "Right as rain, Siria," he

whispered. He reached up and took her hand, squeezing it hard. "Remember . . ."

It was easy to read his mind. He'd said it so many times: *It's the rescue I love, Siria. It's making a difference that helps me want to do this.*

"I love you, Pop." How odd her voice sounded.

An EMT put boards around Pop's leg, shaking his head a little. Siria's own knees were shaking. She sank down next to him, and Danny's arm went around her. "He'll be all right. We'll just take him to the hospital and they'll check him out."

The crowd was leaving now. Willie wound up the hose and the engines pulled away. Mrs. Byars leaned in, her eyes soft. "I could take Siria home with me."

Siria shook her head. "I'm going with him."

Izzy nodded. "Of course she is." Pop smiled a little. "You heard my girl," he told Mrs. Byars, who smiled back.

Easy as that.

They slid the stretcher into the ambulance and Siria climbed up and squeezed into the small space across from Pop.

She kept his hand in hers as the sirens began again, and watched his eyes closing as the ambulance pulled out. He didn't even ask what she'd been doing outside in the middle of the night.

✦

The lounge next to the emergency room was filled with firefighters, all there for him. Siria waited with them, Izzy's arms around her.

At last, the doctor crouched in front of her. "Lucky guy, your dad! No fracture! Bad bruising. Sprains. A broken rib that we've bound up. Nothing major, but we'll keep him here for a day or two. We have to take good care of our firefighters."

She and Izzy followed the doctor back to a cubicle. Pop was asleep and there was color in his cheeks now. He had a clear plastic tube in his nose. "That's oxygen," the doctor said. "Perked him right up."

Siria kissed Pop's forehead and wiped a bit of grit from his cheek. He didn't open his eyes; he was still sleeping.

"Time to go home, honey," Izzy said.

They walked back to the firehouse and stopped in the kitchen for a hot chocolate. Siria had never been there so late. The dormitory door was open, so she could see a row of beds with clean sheets and folded blankets. And right now, it was peaceful. Smoky, the little black cat, sat on the table, half asleep, her tail around her.

"Nobody wants her," Willie said.

"I do," Izzy said. "She's mine now."

"Another rescue," Siria said.

Izzy nodded. "Exactly. That's our job. And this cat will curl up with me on cold nights."

They drove the few blocks to the apartment house in Izzy's car. No one had asked Siria what she was doing in the street in the middle of the night.

Without thinking, she blurted out: "I was chasing you."

Izzy pulled into an open spot in front of the apartment house. "I know." She turned and patted Siria's hands. "I always knew you were there."

She knew!

Siria took a breath. "Does Pop—"

Izzy shook her head. "Just me. You chased your father and I chased you. Every time. As soon as the engine pulled in, I threw off my gear and went to your building to watch as you pedaled in, to be sure you were safe."

She touched Siria's hair. "You belong to us. Besides . . ." She hesitated. "My father was a firefighter, too. His firehouse was far away in the Bronx. I couldn't chase him; I couldn't even hear the sirens. But I was always worried."

At last Siria was crying: for Pop, and because Izzy had been there all the time. Crying because of Douglas, and because she was so afraid he'd set another fire. She was so tired, and how good it felt to let the tears come.

"You're rescuing me," she told Izzy after a few minutes, just able to get the words out.

Izzy gave her a crooked smile. "You and the cat."

Siria reached out to Izzy, smelling the smoke in her hair, seeing the sudden tears in her dark eyes. How would Izzy fit into the make-believe family she and Laila wished for? Maybe an angel. Almost a mother.

"Your pop is really going to be all right," Izzy said. "He's strong and quick. He rolled away from that board—it caught only his side and his leg. It could have been much worse."

Siria nodded uncertainly.

"We're trained, Siria. We know what we're doing. You have to believe that. He'll be home for Christmas. And we'll celebrate."

They hugged again, and then Siria slid out the door. This time she'd remembered her key.

Izzy rolled down the window. "I'm off tomorrow. Want to go Christmas shopping?"

"I do," Siria called back. She went upstairs and tiptoed past Mimi, asleep on the couch.

She didn't bother hanging on the door, but snuggled under the quilt, feeling her feet begin to warm. Imagine! Izzy had known all the time.

"Home for Christmas," she whispered.

From the corner of her window, she could see clouds like pillows covering most of the night sky, but here and there was the pale twinkle of a star.

It was almost as if Mom were looking down at her, telling her not to worry. Pop would be all right. Douglas would stop setting fires. And somehow that poor dog would find food and a place to live.

She wished she could believe it.

CHAPTER 13

Orange flames shot out of a window high over Siria's head. Boards crashed onto the cement below, sending up swirls of dust. "Don't go up the ladder! Stay with me!" she called. "I don't want to be alone."

Her eyes flew open and she sat up in bed.

Just a dream. Only a dream.

No. Not a dream. It had happened: the flames, the ladder, Pop.

Not a piece of cake after all.

She made herself think of Izzy. *We know what we're doing. Home for Christmas.*

Mimi appeared in her bedroom doorway in her wool bathrobe. "Dear child. I just turned on the radio. Your father was hurt last night." She leaned over the bed and ran her hand over Siria's hair.

"He's in the hospital," Siria whispered.

Poor Mimi, so worried about the two of them, didn't even ask how Siria knew. "I'm going downstairs to my place for a few things," Mimi said. "I'll be back to stay with you for as long as you need me."

Siria gave her a quick kiss; then she half slept, dreaming that she and Douglas were down at the creek. Douglas held matches in his hand, laughing.

She woke with tears on her cheeks. The dream had seemed so real: Douglas with his red hair and that baseball hat, freckles covering his face.

"How could you!" she whispered.

The bell rang. It had to be Laila. She always left her finger on the button, listening to the sound of the chimes.

Siria padded to the door, wiping her face with her pajama sleeve.

"I saw Mimi in the hall," Laila said. "She told me about your father. Poor Pop. Poor Siria."

"You're such a good friend, Laila." Siria could hardly get the words out.

"A sister," Laila said.

"Yes."

Laila hesitated. "What are you going to do about Douglas? And the fires?"

Siria heard the fierceness in her own voice. "I have to watch every minute. If Douglas sets one more fire, I'll be there to put it out."

"Laila?" her mother called from downstairs.

"Have to go," Laila said. "Sorry, Siria, so sorry about everything."

"And there's the phone." Siria went into the living room. Sun streamed in the window and rivers of melting snow slid down the pane. She glanced at the clock, half the morning gone. She picked up the phone.

"How's my star girl?" Pop! Sounding almost normal, even happy.

"Are you all right?"

"Fine, Siria, and the security guards are, too. There's just a little pain when I move my side or my leg. But I'll be with you before you know it, eating Mimi's butter cookies." He paused. "Don't worry. I'll be home for Christmas."

"Izzy said that." Siria remembered that once she'd asked him to think about having a farm somewhere upstate, far from the fire department and danger. They'd grow corn and potatoes; they'd have an apple tree with branches that hung over a front porch. Pop had run his hand over her shoulders. "We're fine here. Just fine."

"Home soon," she whispered as he said good-bye, sounding sleepy again.

Now Mimi pushed a suitcase into the living room and came in to see her. Her face was soft and her gray hair was pushed back with a scarf.

"I overslept," Siria said.

Mimi made an *it's not important* sound with her lips.

"Sit on the couch. I'll fix you an omelet with tomatoes and onions. Maybe there's a little ham in the refrigerator."

"Thanks! Terrific," Siria said. "I'm starving."

It was true. How could that be, with Pop in the hospital, and Douglas . . .

Oh, Douglas!

In the kitchen, Mimi pushed aside a tray of cookies to work on the omelet. While she waited, Siria ate four or five chocolate chip cookies.

She ate the omelet then and wondered about the dog. Where was he? Had he found something to eat?

Izzy came in next, smelling of outside cold and almond shampoo. She smiled, her eyes crinkled, and Siria had to smile with her. Once she'd seen Izzy cry when someone was hurt at a fire. Her tears had been silver, brimming in her eyes.

"We could take a quick trip to the hospital," Izzy said.

"Yes!" Siria said. "Let's go."

"I'll wrap a package of cookies for him," Mimi said. "And maybe you'll take the rest to the firehouse."

"Gladly," Izzy said with that great smile. "I'll pick them up for the house later."

Siria slid into her jacket; then they took the elevator down to the lobby. Douglas's mom was waiting to go up. "Sorry about your pop," she said. "And where have you been the last few days? We've missed you."

Siria swallowed. What could she say? "I've missed you, too." It was true. She missed Douglas. She missed his whole family.

She and Izzy walked the few blocks to the hospital. It seemed much closer in the daylight.

Pop was awake when they opened the door to his room. His eyes lit up when he saw them. Siria went closer to kiss him. She sat on the edge of his bed, careful not to hurt him.

They munched on Mimi's chocolate chip cookies. "The best," Pop said. They talked about the fire then, and about Christmas coming. "I'll have a few days off until I'm fit again." His hand went to his side.

And Izzy said, "We have to go. Time to buy some Christmas presents."

✦

They raced for the bus to the mall. Once in their seats, Izzy pulled out a pad. "Let's make a list."

"A knitting bag for Mimi," Siria said. "And shaving stuff for Pop."

Izzy laughed. "How original."

"I wish I could think of something wonderful."

"We'll look high and low," Izzy said.

"There's Danny, and Willie, and Jesse."

"Christmas candy," Izzy said.

Laila was harder. But wait. Hadn't Laila mentioned fish in a tank? Siria closed her eyes. Yes. She'd give her a Siamese fighting fish, blue or purple, with a gently waving tail.

What would Christmas morning be like this year? Pop always made French toast and bacon that sizzled in the pan before they opened the presents under the tree. Would he be all right for that?

"Anyone else?"

"There's you."

"I'd put a new apartment down for myself," Izzy said. "Mine is cold and damp, and there isn't a kid in the whole building."

"You have me."

Izzy squeezed her hand. "Oh, I know that. I do."

They were quiet for a moment. Then Siria began. "I was looking at Pop's book about arson."

"So many stories!" Izzy said.

Siria leaned forward. "Tell one."

Izzy smiled. "One summer there was a kitchen fire, a steaming hot day. It was so hot that it was hard to move in our turnout gear." She shook her head. "Neighbors blamed the man who lived in the house. They believed he set it."

"He set fire to his own kitchen?"

"He'd left a row of glasses on the windowsill. The sun's rays sent the heat up so high that the glasses exploded, one by one. It was your father who saw the char on the glasses, and the fire marks near them. So it wasn't arson at all. Sometimes people jump to conclusions."

Siria sat back. And sometimes people were right.

The bus slowed down. Almost as if she knew what Siria was thinking, Izzy tapped her on the shoulder. "Don't forget Douglas."

Siria answered carefully. "I'll think about that."

That Christmas long ago. Were they five that year? They might have been six. Douglas had made her a necklace out of strips of colored paper. She'd worn it every day until it had fallen apart. And even then she'd kept it in her dresser drawer.

She followed Izzy off the bus. She hoped Izzy wouldn't notice the tears in her eyes.

CHAPTER 14

It was getting dark; silver-gray clouds covered the sky. Siria shrugged into her jacket. She'd meant what she'd said to Laila about Douglas. She'd follow him, watching.

But first, the dog. Had he made it back to the basement, or was he still out somewhere? Caught, or wandering around? Hungry?

"I'll be back," she called to Mimi, and went down to the third floor. Douglas's brother Kevin was coming out, and she stood at the open elevator door. "Where's Douglas?"

Kevin shrugged. "Watching TV."

She tried to think of how to ask . . . what to say.

But Kevin didn't get into the elevator with her. He took the stairs. "Ruined the kitchen," she thought she heard him say.

The elevator door closed and she pressed the button for the basement, her mouth dry.

The dog wasn't in the basement or outside in the alley.

So, Douglas.

She'd go back upstairs and sit on the fourth-floor landing, hidden, waiting for him to come out.

She sat there, halfway between Douglas's floor and the fifth floor. Looking up, she could see that the door to the empty apartment was open. She'd take a quick look.

Someone had left a window open in the living room, and the wind had scattered swirls of snow on the floor and a piece of rug. An empty water bottle was on the sill. It reminded her of Izzy's story about the glasses exploding on a hot summer day, and people believing the owner had set the fire.

She wandered through the rest of the apartment. The bedrooms were like hers and Pop's. The bathroom tile was green instead of white, and there was a long crack in the mirror.

She was staring at her two half faces when she heard the outside door close. She tried not to breathe as she crept into the corner behind the open door, her hand to her mouth.

How could she explain if she was caught?

Above her head, the cracked mirror reflected the world outside. Everything was divided in half, the white hills, the frozen creek, someone running along the edge wearing a dark green jacket.

Had Douglas left his apartment? So quickly?

All was quiet now, no footsteps, not a sound. She pushed the bathroom door with one finger, waited, then ran through the apartment. Someone must have closed the door from the outside.

She'd go after Douglas. Now.

She opened the door again, not quite closing it, and skittered down the stairs and outside.

By the time she reached the creek, huge flakes were falling and it was almost dark. Was someone crying? She stood entirely still, listening, but the wind was strong and it was impossible to be sure.

The sound stopped. She walked along the edge of the creek, climbing over the slippery rocks, and heard a soft whine on the other side of the creek, close to the pipe. It was the dog. She put one boot out, touching the ice, tapping to see if it would hold her weight. But even if she went through, the water would only reach her knees.

Possible. But so cold. She took another step and her foot broke through the ice. Water seeped into her boots, freezing against her toes.

She took a few more steps. And there he was, lying with his feet and legs in the water. "What are you doing here?"

Was he caught somehow?

The chain ran along inside the pipe, and even though she pulled hard, she couldn't get it loose. She yanked off her mittens, dropping them on the ice, and bent down to run her hands along the chain. To one side, through the snow, she caught a glimpse of someone under an evergreen.

A flash of color. Green? A green jacket?

Douglas?

She called out to him. "I see you."

There was a shower of snow from the branches as the person moved.

"Douglas?"

The dog trembled beside her.

It wasn't Douglas. She could see that. Someone taller than Douglas, bigger. But wearing his green jacket.

Who?

She tried to free the dog, almost in a panic to get away from there and whoever was watching.

It was too dark to see the chain as it snaked inside the pipe, which was covered with frozen reeds. She pushed herself in, sleeves soaking, shoulders tight against the rusted sides, with just enough room to run her hands around the surface.

She reached out, stretching, searching, until she felt the end of the chain. Her fingers were numb; it was so hard to get it loose.

And someone was watching. Someone who wasn't Douglas.

The chain gave, and she backed out of the pipe, shivering, wet. The dog, shivering too, didn't even realize he was free.

Siria threw her arms around him, glancing over her shoulder. "We're going home."

It was almost as if he couldn't move. How long had he been standing in the water? Somehow, she dragged him out of the creek.

Another shower of snow cascaded through the branches.

Hurry!

She pulled at the dog's chain and began to run. The dog loped after her, and she almost tripped, looking back, righting herself, reaching the avenue, the dog so close she could feel his wet fur against her jeans.

She slapped at her pockets with frosty fingers. No key. But going around to the back of the building was just too much.

Almo sat near the front door, his chair tipped back against the wall, asleep.

Siria knocked at the door until he jumped. The chair banged down as he stood up to let her in. "What's the matter with you?" he asked. "Where have you been? Out in the storm with that dog?"

He kept talking as Siria walked across the lobby, the dog's claws clicking against the muddy tile floor. She rang for the elevator.

What would Mimi say when she saw them?

The doors opened and the dog followed her inside.

She glanced back. Almo was still staring at her and the puddles they'd left on the floor.

CHAPTER 15

A note was propped up next to a tuna fish sandwich and a glass of juice on the kitchen table.

> *Downstairs in my apartment wrapping*
> *presents. Come down if you need me.*
> *Back soon.*
>
> *Love,*
> *Mimi*

Siria dropped half the sandwich on the floor for the dog and wolfed down the other half, still shivering.

Someone was wearing Douglas's jacket.

The dog looked up at her, waiting for more.

She filled a bowl with water and fed him a can of Viennese frankfurters from the back of the cabinet.

He sank down then and closed his eyes.

She thought of Izzy's story again. *People jumping to conclusions.*

Not Douglas.

Maybe not.

Tomorrow, after the snow had stopped, she'd get to the bottom of all this. At least she'd try.

She looked down at the dog, the red sore the rope had rubbed into the dog's neck, the curved ribs under his fur, and the chain wrapped around one paw. How terrible he smelled; how matted his fur felt.

She reached for the scissors in the cabinet and began to hack at the rope. It was thick and wet and took forever before it fell away, and the chain with it.

What else could she do? Suppose she gave him a warm bath?

Why not!

He followed her down the hall to the bathroom and watched, head tilted, as she filled the tub with a couple of inches of warm water. How good it felt to her stiff, cold hands.

She peeled off her wet socks; her feet were red and even colder than her fingers. She turned to see the dog chewing on the towel she'd dropped on the floor.

She leaned forward. "Just jump in. Nothing to it."

He sat back.

She tried to put his paws on the edge of the tub. "Nice in there. Warm and cozy."

It didn't work.

She tried to lift him, but he pushed against her with his large paws, the pads rough and scarred. She slid backward into the tub with him, splashing the tile walls and the floor.

He was ready to scramble out, but she held him and talked softly as she reached for the soap. In one minute, the water was filthy. She was filthy, too, soaked again, and she hadn't even begun to wash him.

She pulled the plug to get rid of the water and turned on the faucet for another couple of inches. She knelt there, scrubbing him with Pop's clean-smelling soap, working at the knots in his fur with her fingers, his fur lighter and curlier as she scrubbed.

Douglas isn't the arsonist. Never mind what Kevin said. Never mind that Douglas loves fires.

I should trust him.

She rinsed the dog, watching the muddy water swirl down the drain until it turned lighter and, finally, clear.

They were both dripping wet as they came out of the tub. The dog shook himself until the whole bathroom was a mess, lines of water running down the walls, the mirror cloudy, puddles all over the floor.

Siria dried him with a towel and reached for a brush in the cabinet under the sink. She kept working at the knots until his fur was smooth. Then she sat back. He seemed like a different dog. His fur was thick and almost a caramel color; his ears felt like velvet. He looked as if he belonged to someone.

If only he belonged to her.

Something kept nudging at her mind. Something about him. He'd been in the movie theater. At the creek. Maybe even the shed. What did that have to do with the fires?

She wrapped a towel around her shoulders and leaned back against the wall. The dog curled up next to her on the mat. For the first time since she'd gone to the creek, she thought about what had happened. She'd rescued him. Siria the shrimp, able to get halfway into that pipe! She'd saved that dog!

If she could do that, maybe she could solve the fire starting.

She put her hand on his head. What would Pop say to a dog?

He'd say no. He'd remind her of guppies in a bowl, or hermit crabs. No fleas, no dog walking in the snow.

But for the first time she knew what Pop meant when he said "The rescue is everything."

She bent over the dog, resting her head on his broad back.

She didn't know how long they slept on the tile floor, but a noise woke her. She stood up and opened the bathroom door.

Mimi's hand was up, ready to knock. Her mouth fell open when she saw the dog asleep on the mat. "Siria!"

He slept on, almost as if he belonged there, in that warm, steamy bathroom.

If only he did.

"The dog can't stay," Mimi said.

"It's late," Siria said. "Just tonight."

Mimi sighed. "Just this night, and that's it! We'll have to take him to the animal shelter, where someone will give him a home."

Siria blinked back tears. The only home she wanted for him was right there with her.

CHAPTER 16

Early Thursday morning, Siria's fingers flew, texting Pop. *Come home, hurry. It's Christmas Eve. We'll have Mimi's cookies and you can work on a new ship.*

Home before you know it, he answered. *Feeling good. Miss you.*

But before he came home, Siria was determined to find out who had set those fires. She bit her lip. She'd have to talk to Douglas, too.

She remembered thinking there was a connection between the dog and the places that had been on fire. What about the movie theater? Maybe she could find a clue there that would tell her what had happened. She threw on her clothes.

The dog watched her from the bed. As soon as she opened the door, he was right behind her. She stopped in the kitchen for a plate of cookies for her teacher, Mrs. Hall. She'd go there first.

She tiptoed past Mimi, asleep on the couch. Outside the sky was almost light. One star still glowed. "Morning star," she breathed. Fresh snow covered the sidewalks, and the sound of shovels scraping it away was everywhere. She waved at Mr. Trencher and the dry cleaner and kept going, block after block. She rang the teacher's bell, left the cookies, and kept going . . .

Past the empty lots . . . past the old factories . . . until she stood in front of the movie theater. Boards covered the front door.

She went around the snowy alley to the back, the dog following. The door was boarded up, too; a Dumpster pushed against the wall. There was no way to get inside.

She twirled around. The dog was gone. Nothing but paw prints in the snow against the wall. They stopped at the Dumpster.

"Hey." She peered into the narrow space between the Dumpster and the wall. More paw prints, but he'd disappeared.

Sideways, she edged her way behind the Dumpster, too.

Her jacket scraped against the wall. There was hardly room to move. Siria the shrimp. No one else could have done that.

Halfway along, she found another door. It was partially open, and the dog was inside. She followed him, scraping her cheek against the molding. The acrid smell of old smoke burned her throat. A dark film had inched its way up the side wall, and the hems of the velvet curtains were shredded. But the rest of the theater was untouched.

The dog ran up the three steps to the stage and the old movie screen, which was torn around the edges, and disappeared again.

How well he knew this place. She climbed the steps. He was sniffing in back of the screen, then stretched himself out, paws extended, eyes closed.

Asleep?

She crouched down next to him. And then she saw it. Such a small thing. The tip of a knife embedded in the wooden floor. It reminded her of the knife she and Laila had tried to use when they wanted to become blood sisters. Not very sharp. And beyond that was a smear of food on the screen and another scrap of green.

It looked as if the food had spurted out of a can.

She covered the knife tip with the green cloth, put it in her pocket, and left the dog to wander through the theater. Nothing else was left, not the pieces of wood or the charred paper. Everything had been cleaned. She climbed to the balcony and looked down.

Mimi would be awake by now, wondering where she was. "Come on, dog," Siria called, and squeezed herself back outside into the daylight.

She slid into the apartment as Mimi was stretching, ready to make breakfast. They ate with the dog under the table. Siria slipped out of her boots and rubbed her feet against his soft fur. What was going to happen to him?

After breakfast, Siria felt Mimi's warm arms around her. "I'm sorry," Mimi said. "Your father will be home soon, and this dog has to go. I'll get my coat. We'll take him to the vet. Maybe he can tell us what to do."

Siria caught her breath.

"Are you paying attention, Siria?"

"I know. I'll walk him first."

Mimi sighed. "Yes, I'll just finish up the dishes."

Siria reached for her jacket and wound a dry scarf around her neck. "Come on, dog," she said softly.

Outside in the hall: "No pound for you," she said. "Suppose no one wants you? You'd be better off in the basement. I'll tell Mimi . . ."

What? She tried to think as they walked around the block a couple of times. Back at the apartment house, Siria brushed snow off her shoulders and the dog shook himself, sending droplets like rain over the floor.

He didn't mind the elevator, but when the doors

opened to the basement, he sat back, front legs gripping the floor.

"You know this place," Siria told him.

He didn't move.

"I'll bring you food. Lots of food. You can go out whenever you like."

It was almost as if he understood her. He turned his head away.

Someone upstairs rang for the elevator; the doors were closing. "Please," she said, even though she knew it was useless. And then she realized they could go upstairs to the empty apartment.

She pressed the button for five.

CHAPTER 17

Inside the apartment, she stood there listening as the dog wandered from the living room toward the bedrooms. What did she hear? The click of his claws against the wood floor. But something else. Was someone whispering? She backed away toward the door, hardly making a sound.

"Who let you in?" the voice said. A boy, talking to the dog.

She had to pass the hallway.

Could he see her?

She tripped over something under her feet, and glanced down. A green jacket.

"Hey!" The voice again.

She ran. Slid out the door. Down the hall. Never mind the elevator. Grabbed the handrail and dashed up the stairs, two at a time.

And rushed inside to Mimi. Safe. Not even thinking of locking the door behind her.

"Where have you been?" Mimi asked. "And the dog?"

Siria sank down on the living room couch. "Gone." She raised her shoulders.

"Ran away? I'm sorry about him," Mimi said. "But maybe it's just as well." Then she smiled. "Izzy is on her way over with a tree. Your father will be here tomorrow."

Siria reached out and danced Mimi around the kitchen. Pop home! Getting better! Sitting in his big chair. "Oh, Mimi. I'll be so glad."

In front of them, the door opened a few inches.

Mimi turned. And Siria . . .

. . . eyes widening.

The dog!

He went past them into her bedroom, Siria thinking, *He acts as if he belongs here. If only he did.*

Then, *How did he get out of that apartment? And who was in there?*

She closed the door and locked it, feeling someone's hand pushing from the other side.

"It's me," Izzy called. She and Almo carried in a tree, smelling of pine and outdoors.

"Happy holidays." Almo took a plateful of cookies they'd saved for him and left.

"We have to hurry," Izzy said. "Ornaments. Presents wrapped. Decorations. Everything just right!" She hugged Siria. "I told you. Home for Christmas."

"He's going to get a surprise." Mimi's eyebrows were raised.

Izzy reached for one of Mimi's butter cookies. "Mmm. Wonderful." She turned to Siria. "A perfect present?"

Siria took a cookie, too. "Maybe not perfect."

"Definitely not perfect," Mimi said. "And definitely not a present."

Siria took Izzy into her messy room. The dog looked up at her from the bed, his great dark eyes like molasses. A patch of quilt was caught in his mouth.

Izzy sank down on the edge of the bed and gently pulled the quilt away. "He's gorgeous. Chewing on things. He can't be more than two or three years old." Izzy's face was plain, but her smile made it beautiful.

"I'm so glad you like him."

"You can't keep him, though. Your father . . ." Izzy broke off.

"Would you take him?"

Izzy put her hand on Siria's head. "Oh, honey, I just took the cat."

Siria went down to the storage room and brought up the boxes of ornaments: her mother's silver Santa Claus, the drawing Siria had made in kindergarten of Pop's shield, glass icicles that shimmered in the light.

She hung garlands in the living room, remembering last year. Douglas had helped her, standing on a ladder. She felt a pain in her chest. *Douglas. Someone setting fires. And the dog. Oh, the dog.*

Siria glanced at Mimi, her voice thick. "This dog would make a wonderful watchdog for someone."

Mimi held up her hands. "Not for me. And not for you. Before your father gets home, we'll have to find a place for him." She shook her head. "Christmas Eve. Everything's closed." Her voice trailed off. "We'll just have to wait."

Siria looked at Izzy.

"Rescued," Izzy said, grinning. "At least for a day."

But so much to worry about.

CHAPTER 18

Siria was being smothered. She couldn't breathe. And what was that strange noise?

She opened one eye. The dog was on top of her, the edge of her pajama sleeve in his mouth.

Siria pulled at her sleeve. "Stop," she said softly. She threw her arms around him. "Christmas. Our last day together." She felt a catch in her throat.

Siria sat up in bed, looking at the star book and the drawings she'd made of Canis Major. All those stars: one ear up, one ear down, a small tail. With a gold crayon she'd marked in the brightest star in the winter sky, Sirius. "I'll call you Major," she said to the dog. "It fits you perfectly."

But there was no time to think about Major. No time to think about anything but Douglas and what she had to do.

Moments later, she was at his apartment door, knocking, banging. Kevin threw the door open, hair poked up, still in pajamas. "It's seven in the morning, Siria."

"What did Douglas do in the kitchen?" she asked.

He blinked. "Set it on fire."

Douglas was standing behind him now. "Not the whole kitchen," he said. "Just a pot, messed up the stove a little. And my mac 'n' cheese is the best. Worth it."

They were both laughing.

"You were cooking?" Siria said.

"Burning," Kevin said.

Douglas was staring at her.

"I thought . . . ," she began, sounding miserable, feeling terrible.

"Don't think," Kevin said. "I'm going back to bed."

"You thought I was setting fires," Douglas said. "How could you believe that?"

She shook her head. "Sorry," she whispered. "I'm really so sorry." And in her mind, *So glad it wasn't you.*

But Douglas's hand was on his door. Before she knew it, he'd closed it, and she was standing in the hallway alone.

They'd never be friends again. No more summers at the creek together, or hanging out on the fire escape watching the snow; no more anything.

And she still didn't know who was setting the fires.

She went back upstairs to see that Mimi had turned on the tree lights in the living room. Everything smelled of Christmas. She stood there wiping her cheeks, while in the doorway, Major wagged his tail. Cookie crumbs dotted his muzzle. The plate of cookies in the kitchen, empty now.

"I'm going to walk the dog," she called to Mimi in the kitchen.

"Are you all right?" Mimi called.

"Sure," she said, trying to make her voice sound normal, happy.

There was barely time to walk him, feed him, and settle him in her room before the apartment door opened and Pop called, "Siria!"

She closed her door and flew out. Izzy and Mimi were guiding Pop to the couch. He sank down, holding his side.

Siria slid in beside him. She and Pop hugged each other, rocking back and forth. "My star," he said. "I've missed you so much."

They opened presents then, red and green wrapping paper littering the floor. Siria had run across the street the night before for shaving cream and that sunny painting at Max's for Izzy.

"Shaving cream," Pop said. "Just what I wanted."

Siria had to smile. There was probably tons of

shaving cream in the linen closet. She was handing Izzy the wrapped picture when she spotted Major in the doorway, tasting Pop's crutches.

Pop smiled. "Your dog?" he asked Izzy.

Mimi hesitated. "Not really."

Siria's heart was fluttering in her throat. Izzy glanced at her and she looked back, pleading.

"You need a dog around here," Izzy said slowly. "Just the way I needed the cat. It's nice to have a pet."

"A real pet," Siria breathed.

Pop laughed. "That's the last thing we need."

Mimi stood at the kitchen door, wiping her hands on a towel. "The child needs this dog." Her voice was firm, her eyes behind her round glasses determined.

Mimi! It was hard to believe.

Siria remembered the almost-real family she and Laila wanted. She had hoped for a dog then, one she could carry in her backpack. But Major was the one she wanted!

Mimi was still talking. "This dog has helped Siria grow up. She's bathed him, fed him, walked him . . ."

Rescued him.

Siria must have said it aloud.

Pop squeezed her shoulder. "Tell me."

She tried to steady her mouth. "He was all alone," she said. "It's so hard to be alone."

Pop took her hand. "I know."

"He had no one to feed him, or take care of him. . . ." She broke off. "Oh, Pop. I love this dog. I've named him Major."

Pop was silent for a moment. "You're named after Canis Major. Your mom loved seeing that constellation every winter. And your star is in his collar."

"Joe, please," Izzy said to Pop.

"She needs . . . ," Mimi began again.

Pop still didn't say anything.

"Besides," Mimi said. "I knitted him a gold collar to match Siria's Christmas gloves. I stayed up last night to do it."

Pop put his arms out and Siria leaned into them.

"Because I was in the hospital I couldn't buy you something new," he said. "But I do have a gift for you, a charm bracelet Mom wore all the time."

Siria had seen the bracelet in a box on his dresser. She loved those charms: a flower, a firefighter's shield, a baby . . .

"Suppose," Pop said, "we go down to Anton's Jewelry next week. We'll buy a dog charm, since Major's going to be yours."

Hers!

Major seemed to know. He sank down at her feet and slept while they opened the rest of their presents.

CHAPTER 19

The morning after Christmas, Siria stood at her bedroom window, holding the bracelet. It had circled Mom's wrist long ago. Mom had touched those small charms, just as Siria did now. And next week there'd be a new charm.

She left the apartment, carrying the little round bowl with its blue-purple fighting fish looking out at the world. Down the steps, carefully, water sloshing. She pressed Laila's bell with her elbow.

Laila opened the door, threw her arms around Siria, and pulled her inside. "Beautiful! I'll name her . . ."

She stared into the bowl, her eyes large behind her glasses. "I'll name her for you: Sister."

They both laughed. "I think it's a male," Siria said.

"All right. Brother." Laila sighed. "The dog," she said then. "Is he yours now?"

Siria nodded. "The one that wandered around. All cleaned up now."

Laila handed her a package. Siria could feel it was a book. "Perfect," she said as she tore off the paper: a book that showed the constellations. "I love it."

She leaned forward. "I found out. Douglas didn't set those fires."

"I'm so glad," Laila said. "We have our brother back for our pretend family."

If only . . .

Siria went back upstairs, thinking about the last present she had to give. She'd seen it in Max's Art Supply Store when she'd bought the painting for Izzy: a model of the *Monitor*, a Civil War ship, ready to put together.

She left Major in her bedroom and went downstairs quickly. She left the package in front of Douglas's door.

He'd know it was from her.

Then she huddled on the fire escape, sitting on her quilt, watching a few flakes of snow drift down, and heard the clang of work boots against the iron steps as Douglas came up toward her.

At first he didn't say anything, and she knew that if she tried to speak, she'd start to cry.

"Your present," he said then. "The *Monitor.* Is that what we've been having? A war?"

"Someone's been setting fires. Wearing your jacket. And I heard Kevin talking about your kitchen." She shook her head. "Your hands all blistered . . ."

He leaned against the brick wall, shaking his head.

"I should have known you wouldn't do something like that."

"Begin again," he said. "The whole thing."

She spoke as slowly as Laila would have. The shed. The movie theater. The creek. She went through all of it, watching his face. He was listening carefully. He always paid attention.

"Where's that piece of cloth?" he asked.

She reached into her pocket and handed it to him, with the knife tip caught inside.

"It's from my jacket. I tore it on the roof. My mother had a fit!" He touched the knife, then squinted up at the snow. "I gave the jacket to my cousin, Kim. She said it was the ugliest thing she ever saw. She'd use it for a play her class was doing."

Kim with the hoop earrings! Siria had seen her somewhere. Was it right after the shed fire?

Had Kim set those fires?

Douglas was thinking that, too; she could see it

in his face. He shook his head. "She's at our grand-mother's today. When she gets back, I'll find out."

Siria nodded, hesitated. "You're my best friend."

"You're mine, too, I guess." He grinned at her.

They sat there thinking. "Maybe we should look at the shed again right away," Siria said. "Maybe she left something in there."

Douglas stood up, slapped his hands together. "We have a lot to do."

Douglas. Friends again.

CHAPTER 20

Clouds scudded across the sky as they waded into the lot, circling the trees. "See?" she said. "Footprints all over the place."

Douglas put his foot into one. "A little bigger than mine. Not much, though." He frowned. "Maybe a teenager. Maybe Kim."

They stopped at the shed door and stood there, listening.

"I don't hear anything," she whispered.

Douglas leaned forward, his head against the door. "All right, then." He shoved it open.

Light filtered in from the spaces between the walls. The room was a mess. The quilt was bunched up in the corner, so filthy it was hard to know what color it had been.

"Someone was living here." Douglas pointed to

the wall. "Probably not since the fire. A small piece of the wall was burned, so the wind comes through. Colder than ever."

He kicked at the quilt. "But this wasn't Kim. She'd never want to live in this mess. Besides, she's afraid of her shadow." He looked down at the quilt. "That was my brother Ashton's a long time ago. Mom threw it out." He grinned. "But Ashton didn't set those fires. He hardly leaves his bedroom, texting, watching TV."

"Let's get out of here."

Douglas closed his eyes. "Who did I see that day? Just Jason and his friend with the tattoo. And yeah, Kim, coming out of Trencher's." He bent down. "Here's something."

Siria leaned over his shoulder. "What?"

"An earring." Douglas grinned at her. "A star. Here's your fire starter."

"Mine!" She scooped it up. "But I didn't—"

"I know that. I wouldn't blame you."

"Sorry," she said again, knowing exactly what he meant.

✦

That night, from her window, Siria watched snow swirling. She saw something a few blocks away and angled her head. An orange glow? Was it another fire? Yes. She had to go out. She had to see.

Pop had gone to sleep early after dinner, and Major slept on the edge of her bed.

In her jacket, Siria waded through the gift wrap they hadn't bothered to clear away from the living room. She scooped up the new gloves Mimi had knitted for her: black with a gold thread running through.

Outside, she listened for the sirens, but everything was quiet, and she couldn't see the fire. She stepped back and tilted her head to look up at her window, to figure out the direction.

Where was it?

She spun around.

That way.

Toward the school.

She walked quickly, quietly, listening to the soft swish of her boots. Overhead, the moon cast shadows on the street. No one was out, and a few lights gleamed from windows. The whole world was home, sleeping. Except for her. And maybe someone who set fires.

The school loomed in front of her, the cement models of the presidents over the door looking weird in the dark. She went into the snowy yard through the open gate.

Dim lights shone from the halls inside. In her classroom, chairs were lined up on the tables. Mrs. Hall's desk was in front, neat now for the holidays, with only the large wooden apple someone had given her for her birthday.

Siria still couldn't see any fire.

Had she imagined it? That ragged orange glow that flickered in the dark?

She trudged around the side of the building where the snow hadn't been shoveled. Litter baskets were lined up against the half-opened door of the small house where lawn mowers were kept.

Four baskets.

And two were on fire!

Small fires, but still . . .

She went closer. Was anyone here, watching her?

The baskets were stuffed with burning newspapers, curling at the edges. It wasn't ordinary school litter like old notebooks, loose leaf or homework sheets. Someone had wadded up newspapers, shoved them into the baskets, and set them on fire.

Who?

Kim, back from her grandmother's house?

Who else might it be?

Siria pulled off the new wool gloves so they wouldn't get wet and laid them on the steps behind her. She heaped handfuls of freezing snow on top of the baskets, listening to the sizzle as they hit the flames, her fingers growing numb.

She heard something. Someone coming around the side of the building? Coming toward her? The footsteps were almost silent, just the faintest crunch in the snow.

She told herself it was her imagination. Really. No one was there.

She couldn't make herself turn; she couldn't move. She looked past the litter baskets to the end of the building, to the fence.

There was no way out.

She picked up an icy chunk of snow, ready to throw it, and then she did turn, arm raised . . .

To see Major, trotting up, panting a little.

She dropped the chunk of ice and slid down in the snow. "Oh, Major," she breathed. "I'm so glad it's you. How did you ever get out?"

He stood over her, licking her cheek, and she put her arms around him. The night was different now, the dark a friendly dark. The dying flames from the litter basket sent a warm glow around them.

After a moment, she put out the rest of the fire. "We can go home," she said. "Home to bed. To our quilt." The quilt was a little chewed; so was the pillow, and even the corner of the rug. But she didn't care.

They plodded along the side of the building, squinting through the falling snow. Siria held one hand on Major's head, the other hand deep in her pocket.

Then Major whined. He took a few steps forward. Someone was there—a boy. He stood in the shadow of the building, head bent, and he was watching her.

She couldn't see his face, but it was a teenager, much taller than she was. He wore sneakers and Douglas's green jacket. He turned, stepped back, raced along the wall toward the Cyclone fence, and was gone.

It was someone she knew. But who?

She waited long minutes, afraid to follow, afraid to get too close. And next to her, Major was quiet. He was no watchdog!

But why had he whined? Did he know who had been there? Did he know who was setting those fires?

She went through the gate with Major at her side and ran up the avenue, almost flying, looking over her shoulder. The street was empty; there wasn't even a car in sight.

Across the way, Max's had a new painting in the window: apple trees with a froth of white blossoms. And at Trencher's, the Christmas lights still flashed, reflecting off the snowy street, and the Santa Claus reached out. She stopped.

The Santa Claus's hands.

Her gloves were still in the snowy schoolyard. Mimi's beautiful Christmas gloves!

"We have to go back, Major. But it's all right. I think he's gone."

If only she could be sure!

The wind blew around them, pushing them along. She couldn't wait to be in her warm bedroom, snuggled next to Major.

"Come on. We have to do this."

He followed her back down the avenue and in through the schoolyard gate. She could smell the charred newspapers as they neared the litter baskets.

Her gloves weren't there. Not on the snow. Not in front of the little storage house, not blown up against the fence.

Someone had taken them.

CHAPTER 21

On Sunday, Siria walked Major around the block a few times, wearing her old mittens.

What would Mimi say about the missing gloves? After all that work! She'd feel terrible.

Siria felt terrible, too.

Hapy New Year was written on the wall of the elevator, almost covering *Mery Christmas*. In her apartment, something smelled delicious. Sausages? Bacon?

"I'm so glad you're home, Pop," Siria said, shrugging off her jacket.

Pop hobbled back and forth between the counter and the stove, a crutch under one arm. "It's great to be here. Hospital food is not like Willie's meals at the firehouse." He turned the bacon he was frying and popped up the bread in the toaster. "It isn't even half as good as my own poor cooking."

Siria picked out a can of beef for Major. *Dogs eat beef like crazy*, Mike had said.

"Where's that can opener, anyway?" she muttered.

Pop smiled. "Mom tried to use a knife sometimes."

"Did it work?"

"What do you think?"

"Guess not." She stopped, looking down at the drawer, remembering the knife tip she'd found in the theater, picturing the spray of food against the screen.

Someone had been eating there. No kitchen. No can opener.

Was that what it was all about? Someone had been living in the shed, trying to keep warm? Then in the theater? Then . . .

"What's going on in that head of yours?" Pop asked.

Siria broke off a piece of toast. "Can't talk, have to eat." She dumped Major's beef into a bowl and finished her breakfast. "I'm on my way to see Douglas." She patted Major. "Stay here. Eat everything in sight."

"Chew everything, you mean," Pop said over his

shoulder. "Wait until you see the couch cushion. The stuffing is coming out. We need to get him a bone."

"Eek." She gave Pop a kiss and headed for the third floor.

Ashton stuck his head out the door. "He's up on the roof."

She headed for the roof, but the door wouldn't budge.

She banged hard and heard Douglas's voice. "Wait a minute."

He opened the door, just a crack. "What?" He wore a new wool hat over his corkscrew hair.

"What are you doing?"

"Sorry, don't need you." He grinned. "Go away."

She tried to peer through the opening, but she could see only a bit of gray sky, and Laila, bending over something. "What's going on?"

Douglas came into the hall, pulling the door closed behind him. "You'll see."

Was it the star shelter! Her birthday present?

"But I want to tell you something," he said. "Kim is back. She didn't set those fires. She wore the jacket in the school play and then left it in the costume box." He shrugged. "Someone at the play must have taken it. She thought she saw Jason, the delivery boy."

"And he was at the schoolyard last night."

"Really?" Douglas tilted his head. "Later. I can't talk anymore. I have work to do."

"I could help."

"You can't see what we're doing. . . ." He squinted. "Not until New Year's Day."

So it really was the star shelter. A surprise for her. She leaned against the wall, feeling joy in her chest. She whispered it to herself: *Douglas. Laila. The star shelter.*

She went back downstairs. Mimi was in the hall, hands on her hips. "Where is that delivery boy? I've ordered the makings of a good dinner."

"I'll go," Siria said, her hands behind her back.

Mr. Trencher was behind the counter, helping someone.

He smiled when he saw her. "Siria, did you get everything you wanted for Christmas?"

"A dog."

The shopper picked up her packages. "That's the best present."

Siria nodded. "Mimi sent me. . . ."

"I'm sorry. I know she's waiting." Mr. Trencher took a list out of his pocket. "Just let me find everything." He went to the back of the store and pulled out bunches of carrots, string beans, and broccoli. He took meat from another bin, then called back, "She wants a giant bag of kibble. Guess that's for the new dog."

Siria leaned on the counter. Kibble. Major would love it.

Mr. Trencher piled food on the counter. "You might have to make two trips with all this," he said. "I'm sorry. I can't leave the store."

"It's all right," she said. "It's fine. Is Jason off for the holidays?"

"That boy. Lazy! And food is missing, even dog food. Dog food! Not a can of beef left. Can you imagine? I fired him. Told his friend I didn't want to see him in here anymore."

Jason. It had been Jason all the time.

She picked up the bag of kibble and one of the other bundles. She asked as slowly as Laila would. "Do you know where Jason lives?"

Mr. Trencher leaned on his elbows. "Somewhere near the school." He waved his hand. "Just past the old shed."

Siria nodded. As soon as she brought the groceries upstairs, she was going to find him.

CHAPTER 22

Siria put the groceries away. Jason was a lot bigger than she was, a lot stronger. But being small had helped her before. She'd slid into the pipe to free the dog, edged her way into the movie theater.

She'd be as tough as she had to be. She took a breath.

Maybe.

He'd probably stolen her Christmas gloves. She'd get them back, and tell him this was the end of the fire starting.

After lunch, Pop lay on the couch, napping, and she snapped on Major's red leash. "Come on," she whispered. "You'll make me braver than I am."

Laila and her mother were in the elevator. "Merry Christmas," Laila said. "We're on our way to my aunt's house for more presents!"

There was a small dot of gold paint on Laila's cheek. From painting the star shelter? Siria smiled. Her birthday was only a few days away!

Outside, she and Laila waved as they went in opposite directions.

Where would she begin to look for Jason? The shed? She took Major along to the empty lots. The door was open, banging in the wind, the old quilt still bunched up in the corner. No fresh footprints in the snow.

Next they wandered around the school. The litter baskets were still there; one had tipped over, and blackened newspaper blew across the yard.

The janitor came outside. "Do you miss school so much you have to come on the holidays?" He glanced at the baskets and frowned.

Siria shook her head. "I didn't do that."

He nodded. "You're a good kid, I know that." He reached down and gave Major a pat.

"I'm looking for Jason," she said.

"The delivery boy?"

She nodded.

"Two kids always together," the janitor said. "I even mix them up sometimes. Mike is the other one. I see him around sometimes with his dog, but not one like yours. His is a mess. The boy really doesn't take care of him."

Siria froze. She could hardly get the words out. "A dog that looks like a wolf?"

"Exactly." He nodded and ran back up the steps.

Siria waved, tugged gently on Major's leash, then left the schoolyard.

The janitor called after her. "I don't know about Jason. But I think I saw Mike down at the creek. A lot of kids are ice-skating."

She'd have to start there. Mike would know where Jason was.

But Major wasn't hers. The words thudded in her chest. He belonged to Mike? How could she give him up?

Major loped along beside her as she walked toward the sledding hills and the creek. He loved it. He stopped to bite an old leaf that had blown up against the curb. He pushed a lump of snow with his nose. And he looked up at her, almost as if he were saying *What fun this is!*

And there was Jason, ahead of her, ice skates slung over his shoulder.

"Wait!" Siria called after him.

He turned, wearing a puffy navy-blue jacket and blue leather gloves.

"I want to talk to you about the fires," she said.

He shook his head. "What fires?"

She stepped away from him, trying to make

herself stand there, to stand tall. "The ones you set."

He raised his hands to his chest, his face shocked. "Not me. Never me."

"Where's the green jacket?"

He frowned. "What's this about?"

"Did you take a jacket?"

"Sure. I gave it to Mike. He was cold, his own jacket was thin, worn out."

It flashed through her head. In the schoolyard. Could it have been Mike watching her?

She closed her eyes. Not Douglas. Not Jason. What was the matter with her? Mike.

"Forget it," she told Jason. She stumbled around him and headed for the creek.

The ice was thicker today, and a bunch of kids were skating. She watched for a while, and then she saw Mike, wearing the torn green jacket. He was sliding around, no skates, but wearing her knitted gloves, so small for him they hung off his hands.

Major saw him, too. He would have run to Mike if she'd let go of the leash. He pulled, whining softly. She tugged back. "Mike!" she called.

He saw her and hesitated. After a moment, he came toward her. "What do you want?"

Major tugged harder at his leash, trying to get to him.

"My father is a firefighter. I don't want him to get hurt. And . . ." Her hands went to her hips. She was yelling now. "You're setting fires. That's arson!"

He came closer. Major, his paws raised against Mike's legs, loved him. She could see that. She'd never felt worse.

"I had to keep warm," he said. "All the snow . . ." He broke off. "The dog looks good."

"No thanks to you."

He bent down, picked up a small stone, and threw it so it skittered across the ice. "Are you going to keep him?"

"Isn't he yours?" Tears filled her throat.

Mike shook his head. "I felt sorry for him. It's hard to keep a dog when you don't have a place to stay. Even that empty apartment Jason found for me didn't last." He rubbed the back of his neck. "Anyway, the dog's all right now." He stared after the stone. "And I'm going home."

She looked over her shoulder toward the houses along the avenue. "Where's that?"

"Pennsylvania."

"Far . . ."

"I had a fight in school and a fight with my parents. So I left. I met up with Jason, a good guy. He helped me find places to sleep. But I miss my mom and my dad. It's too much here. Too cold. I had to set fires to keep warm. Then the dog came along. I had to feed him, too." He bent down to rub Major's head. "I called my family. They'll be glad to see me."

"Pennsylvania? Without the dog."

"I don't have to worry about him anymore."

He was going to let her have Major. He was going far away. Oh, Major. Hers. Really hers.

He patted the dog gently. "I was too big to get him out of the pipe. I was glad when you came along."

She nodded. "But you stole cans of food from Trencher's. A jacket. A quilt."

He began to laugh. "The quilt? Right out of the garbage, in case the dog wanted to sleep in the shed. The food—I'll pay Trencher back."

He picked up another stone, larger now, and sent it after the first one. "Good thing you have him now."

"One more thing. How did you open all those cans? For you? For Major?"

He raised one shoulder. "Had a knife. It broke. I stole an opener from Trencher. I'll pay him back for that, too. As soon as I can." He leaned forward. "I'm not a bad guy. I was just so cold and hungry."

She hesitated, then smiled. "And you're wearing my Christmas gloves. I'd give them to you, but my sitter made them. She'd feel bad."

He smiled, too, then yanked them off. "I found them in the snow. They're way too tight."

She pulled them over her fingers, still warm from his hands. "Thanks. I'm glad you're going home."

She leaned down, and held Major's broad face in her hands. "Come on, let's go."

The boy looked back over his shoulder. "Not bad for such a shrimp."

She waved after him. "No, not bad," she said. "Get home safe."

CHAPTER 23

January first: Siria's birthday, and the beginning of a new year!

The night would be clear and cold. Even now, in the late afternoon, she could see a faint dusting of stars. There were millions more she couldn't see. They glowed far away throughout the vast universe. Unseen, like the unicorn constellation Mimi had told her about.

Pop would never know about all that had happened. He'd never know what Siria had done.

But she knew what Mom would want her to do.

How could she do this?

How could she not?

She wandered into the front room. Pop was putting the finishing touches on his latest model.

"I need to talk to you," she said.

"So serious on your birthday?"

She sank down in the chair next to him and told him all of it. Fire chasing. Fire setting. How Mike had gone back to Pennsylvania. The only thing she didn't tell him was that Izzy had been watching over her. That wasn't her story to tell.

And then she waited, wondering what he'd say.

He began, and she knew most of it. He talked about the risks she'd taken. The danger, outside at night, not telling him sooner. What was arson and what wasn't.

But he surprised her. "You grow more like your mother every day. And I shouldn't tell you this, but she probably would have done exactly what you did." He thought about it. "I'm glad the boy has gone back home. I'm glad this is the end of it."

He held up his hand. "No more fire chasing, right?"

She nodded, looking at his blue eyes, his dear freckled face, and couldn't speak. She reached out and hugged him hard.

CHAPTER 24

The birthday feast! Mimi had made a huge turkey with raisin stuffing, which Siria rescued just before Major reached the table. Laila had made place cards and invitations to the star shelter after dinner.

Everyone was there. Izzy with her cat, Smoky, who hid from Major under the couch. Mimi, of course. Douglas and Laila, who said they couldn't wait to show Siria what they'd done, and Pop . . .

Pop looked happy, his leg almost healed, wearing a Velcro brace.

Izzy leaned over and squeezed Siria's hand. "My Christmas painting hangs over my fireplace, warm and sunny, reminding me of you."

And Pop put his arms around her just before they sat down. "From now on, I'll text you after every fire so you won't worry."

And best of all, he'd discovered he really liked dogs, even though Major had chewed up a piece of the living room rug, the front room curtain, and one of Pop's knitted slippers. But Mimi was halfway through a new one. And Major now had chew toys to keep him busy most of the time.

The birthday cake was strawberry with swirls of vanilla icing and too many candles to blow out in one breath. Then, after dinner, they went up to the roof with flashlights glowing. "Here's our surprise," Laila said, and Douglas nodded. "For Siria."

She drew in her breath. The star shelter was a great square of wood painted midnight blue, with gold stars here and there. Inside were old pillows and blankets.

It was perfect for all of them squeezed in together, out of the wind.

Siria was the warmest, because Major had draped himself across her lap.

With blankets around them, they watched the sky, and Pop pointed at the three stars of Orion's belt.

The Hunter with his sword, ready to fight.

And then, at last, Siria saw the long Y of Canis Major and the dazzling star Sirius.

"Your star, Siria," Pop said.

She drew in her breath. Behind her, Laila patted her shoulder. Mom's bracelet circled her wrist, and the star book was in her pocket, making Mom feel close.

She looked around at all the faces: Pop, Izzy, Mimi smiling at her, Laila and Douglas, Major sound asleep on her lap.

Not a make-believe family. Not even an almost family. They were all hers.

No one knew what was far out there in the universe, circling the sun, circling the earth. Wasn't there a story about that in Mom's book? Siria could almost see it on the last page in Mom's neat handwriting.

They watched the stars for a long while, then went downstairs. Siria looked through the little book until she found what she was looking for.

Maybe Mom was telling her something.

Mom, somewhere high in the heavens, looking out for her.

SIRIUS

Long ago, astronomers noticed something unusual about Sirius. The star didn't sail across the sky in a straight line as they expected it to do.

It took years to find out why.

Sirius wasn't alone. A genuine white dwarf star traveled with her, the two circling the sky together. One looking after the other.

The white star couldn't be seen, not even by Sirius.

But it was there.

Sirius was never alone.

CHAPTER 25

The holidays were over; school would start again tomorrow. It was Pop's first night back to work, and in the living room, Mimi was crocheting a rug. Already it covered her lap and cascaded to the floor. If she kept it up, it might cover the whole apartment house.

Siria climbed into bed and Major stretched out on her feet.

Major had loved Mike, the fire starter. Siria wasn't sorry. Izzy had said once it was good to love as many people as you could.

Siria heard sirens and sat up, but Major didn't move. She sank back down, sliding her feet underneath the dog, and pulled the quilt up higher around her. Pop would text as soon as they'd put out the fire.

Pop and the firefighters really didn't need her. They looked out for each other.

She closed her eyes, her hand on her iPhone.

How great it was to lie here, cozy. Not to sneak out in the dark, into the cold, the snow.

It was a whole new year.

ABOUT THE AUTHOR

Patricia Reilly Giff is the author of many beloved books for children, including the Kids of the Polk Street School books, the Friends and Amigos books, and the Polka Dot Private Eye books. Several of her novels for older readers have been chosen as ALA-ALSC Notable Children's Books and ALA-YALSA Best Books for Young Adults. They include *The Gift of the Pirate Queen; All the Way Home; Water Street; Nory Ryan's Song*, a Society of Children's Book Writers and Illustrators Golden Kite Honor Book for Fiction; and the Newbery Honor Books *Lily's Crossing* and *Pictures of Hollis Woods. Lily's Crossing* was also chosen as a *Boston Globe–Horn Book* Honor Book. Her most recent books are *Gingersnap, R My Name Is Rachel, Storyteller, Wild Girl*, and *Eleven*, as well as the Zigzag Kids series. She lives in Connecticut.

Patricia Reilly Giff is available for select readings and lectures. To inquire about a possible appearance, please contact the Random House Speakers Bureau at rhspeakers@randomhouse.com.